PROFESSOR ZADDY

A Potomac Falls Novel

K.L. Hall

B. Love Publications

Synopsis

A promiscuous college senior.
A handsome professor with secrets.
A kidnapping and shocking campus crime.

When I stepped onto the campus at West Bridge University four years ago, all I wanted to do was get my degree.

Now, I'm one class away from walking across the stage in the spring.

Graduation is so close I can taste it.

That's the only reason I signed up for Professor Hill's erotic poetry class. Well, not the *only* reason.

His seductive cocoa brown eyes, salt and pepper beard, and sexy tattoos precede him.

I never intended for him to become my muse behind every poem, every fantasy.

One glance across the lecture hall and a moment alone after class is all it took to make him mine.

But there are consequences to breaking the rules, and my all-consuming desire lands me in heart-pounding danger.

How was I to know the debonair, well-dressed professor was living a double life as a drug kingpin?

I guess that's why they say some men are off-limits for a reason.

Professor Zaddy is a standalone forbidden professor-student novel based in Potomac Falls.

"Nobody fucks you better than a nigga you ain't supposed to be fuckin'."

Warning!

PROLOGUE

T he Student

Ava Newman

"Nine-one-one, what's your emergency?"

The phone trembled in my clammy hand as the operator's voice crackled through the receiver.

"I-I'm a West Bridge University student... and t-there's a f-fire!" My voice quivered as I stumbled over my words. "P-please s-send help!"

"Okay, calm down. I need you to stay on the line and tell me where you are. Is the fire on campus?"

"Yes. On the north side of campus."

"I'm putting in the request right now to have the Potomac Falls Fire Department and campus police dispatched to your location."

"Okay."

"Stay on the line, okay?"

"Okay."

"What's your name?"

"Ava. Ava Newman."

"Okay, Ava. Can you describe the fire for me? Is it a small fire or a big one?"

My heart galloped like a wild stallion against my ribcage. "The flames are huge, and the smoke is thick."

"Are you inside the building?"

"No. I-I was walking on campus, and I saw the flames."

"Do you know if there is anyone inside?"

The crackling symphony of flames surrounding me amplified, drowning out my sobs as

I watched the flames dance with an insatiable hunger, licking at the walls that pulsed with secrets I knew I had no choice but to take to my grave.

"I-I don't know."

"Ma'am, are you hurt?" the operator probed.

I looked down at my bruised wrist. "No."

Like silver tears, raindrops cascaded from the sky, attempting to quench the inferno. But the fierce orange and yellow flames persisted, their dance intensified by the downpour. I inched further away from the building as the thick smoke billowed, obscuring my vision and setting fire to my lungs. It clung to my skin and clothes.

A few minutes passed before my ears were piqued by sirens wailing in the distance. It was a hopeless symphony. They'd arrive to see there was no one to be saved. The darkness tightened its grip on me as negative thoughts crept up to the forefront of my mind. *Will they arrive and think I did this?*

In that suspended moment, I found myself trapped between worlds: the one where I was just a college student trying to make it to graduation day and the other where I was a witness to an unspeakable horror. My skin prickled with fear, and my senses heightened as the sirens grew closer. I couldn't unhear their gurgling breaths, their final pleas for forgiveness.

"Ava, are you still there?" the operator questioned. Her voice cut through the fog, drawing me back to our conversation.

"Y-yes," I whispered. "I'm here."

"Good. Stay with me. The authorities are almost there. Do you hear the sirens?"

"Y-yes. I hear them."

I waited, wrapped in the silence as raindrops collided with the searing heat. My heart thumped in sync with the approaching sirens. The taste of tragedy lingered on my tongue as I wondered how many lives would unravel once the news spread like wildfire across campus. The darkness held its secrets, and I was one of them. There was only one pressing thought replaying in my head as the firefighters arrived: *how the fuck did I get myself into this?*

THE STUDENT

*F*our *months earlier.*

The biting cold of January clung to my skin as I stepped onto the snow-dusted campus. My winter break had been a blur of stressful family gatherings, long nights of applying for jobs and grad school by the fireplace, and the anticipation of returning to West Bridge University to graduate in the spring. As a college senior, the new year promised new beginnings.

My breath fogged the air as I gazed at the snow-covered quad. Somehow, the campus seemed smaller, as if it had been shrinking with each passing semester. Either that, or I'd gotten too familiar with the territory over the past four years. I remembered my freshman self, wide-eyed and eager, navigating the labyrinth of a campus. Now, I could trace the familiar paths to the dining hall, the library, and my favorite study nook like the back of my hand. The memories of late-night cram sessions and laughter with classmates made me smile. West Bridge had witnessed my growth—all the triumphs and the stumbles in between. The future loomed—a cocktail of excitement and anxiety.

Graduation was on the horizon, and with it came the *real* world. Job applications, interviews, and the weight of student loans pressed heavily on my mind. I couldn't be the laughingstock of my family. I was the youngest of three girls. Both of my sisters had big-shot careers as veterinarians and speech-language pathologists. I couldn't afford to fall short. I had no idea what was in store after college, but I had to do what I had to do to walk across that stage. But I pushed those thoughts aside, choosing to focus on the crunch of snow under my boots instead.

Going out into the real world meant needing *real* money. I'd saved as much as I could for the past nine months. My scholarship was my lifeline. It eased the financial burden on my parents, and my job as a hall aid provided me with free housing. I was grateful for both. I'd been content with my free, cozy dorm room, but I'd be lying if I said I hadn't grown sick of the smell of instant noodles and laundry detergent. I'd become a big sister to the female first-year students on my floor, offering unsolicited advice, dropping gems on how to survive midterms, and navigating through courses with demanding professors. I worked my ass off for the past four years, burning the midnight oil in the library fueled by caffeine and energy drinks. The least I could do was steer them in the right direction.

But what truly made my pulse quicken was the email I received about my acceptance into an exclusive class. "Topics in the Harlem Renaissance: Erotic Poetry" was an invitation-only course. Professor Augustine Hill was legendary, not to mention handsome as hell. Not only was he a renowned professor with a list of accolades that was a mile long, but he was also the *only* professor on campus who taught the course. Each semester, it ranked as the most sought-after class, with a waiting list three semesters long. His enigmatic smile, genetically blessed build, tattoos, and salt and pepper beard fueled campus gossip. Some said he was a mastermind, others said he was a recluse. His expertise bridged art history, literature, Black culture, and philosophy. His course promised to delve into the hidden layers of creativity, exploring the underworld of erotic art forms during the Harlem Renaissance.

Professor Hill's background was shrouded in mystery. He wasn't on social media, not even LinkedIn. There were no articles about him online or classroom notes from past students from previous semesters. Rumor had it he studied exclusively under reclusive Black artists and philosophers in Europe, unlocking secrets whispered only to a select few. I only needed *one* more class to have enough credits to graduate, and I was glad I'd snagged a seat in his. I planned to be at the front row center every Friday evening from six o'clock to nine-thirty and give Professor Hill my undivided attention.

———

February.

I was hooked the first time I stepped foot into Professor Hill's class. His lectures were spellbinding. His eyes—a warm sienna brown—seemed to see right through me. His baritone voice was like a sonnet wrapped in cashmere, revealing secrets of Black history and eroticism across the lecture hall. I watched in awe as he dissected our history through words, each class a new revelation. His strong brown hands were long-fingered and expressive as he spoke. I imagined them on my skin, mapping constellations of longing over my nipples down to my sweet spot. Like the black tattoos etched into his Tuscan brown skin, his presence lingered like ink stains on my fingertips long after class ended. He weaved literature and philosophy with personal anecdotes, leaving me fiending for the next week. As engaged as I was, his class wasn't for the faint-hearted. Professor Hill demanded rigorous study and pushed creative boundaries.

The crisp bite of the February air seeped through the cracks of my frost-kissed window inside my dorm room. I stared at the blinking cursor on my laptop, the blank document craving confession. I pulled my weed pen away from my lips, letting the smoke filter through my nostrils as my imagination ran wild. Soon after, words spilled onto the screen in purple font, bleeding into one erotic verse after another. I wrote of his eyes, the color of cognac, and how they dissected my soul, revealing intimate layers of myself I didn't even know existed. How I

yearned for him to dip his quill into my inkwell, ring on his finger be
damned.

I Fell in Love with a Poet
Ava Newman

I fell in love with a poet once,
And I don't know; maybe it was the way,
His words gripped my waist and blew in my ears
Like the sea whispering to a seashell.

Or maybe it was the way his tongue ripped through
His lips to drip verses of lust onto my vulnerable flesh.
The way he thrust syllables together to
Flow in unison like juices from my personal nectar tree,
And kissed rhymes timed to perfection.

My lipstick stains tattoo the pages of his notebook,
He starts... raspy, groans submerge from his diaphragm,
As his tongue flirts religiously with my inner thigh... I mean thoughts.

His oral, uh, aura... clenches the bed sheets of my brain,
And his breath, humid yet sweet, graces the nape of my neck,
Bouncing ballads off my breasts,
While honey dripping haikus slide down to my navel.

But that's just the first verse...

His stanzas stand like kickstands on bikes,
As his iambic pentameter penetrates and intoxicates,
All while speeding up the pace,
Spitting words out faster and faster,
Free verses of flesh bending together like broken rules

Until we both...

Take flight, moon bouncing on clouds of ecstasy
With nothing but caressed couplets
And moist metaphors between us.

The afterglow of alliteration
And sticky similes, birth smiles on both of our faces.

He asks, "Are you up for round two?"
And begins licking limericks from my lips.

Tides roll in as he turns pages,
Shamelessly sending shockwaves of sonnets through my body.
Blank verses bend me over,
His hands entangled in my hair like epics of Homer from the Odyssey

As I rain quatrains and orgasm to onomatopoeias.

· · ·

Yeah, I fell in love with a poet once.
But if he fucked you this good, could you blame me?

I rested my back against my pillows and shifted slightly, immediately feeling the wetness of my panties after writing about my professor. He'd become the object of my most intimate fantasies. Ever since the first night I spent in his class, I'd been used to the waterworks between my thighs whenever a thought of him surfaced.

Each of my masturbation sessions ended with me screaming his name to the heavens as my back arched high enough to sneak a peek at Jehovah himself. My phone jolted me from reverie, and the sweet thoughts of my man crush dissolved. The screen illuminated with Lincoln's name. We'd been dancing a delicate waltz since the previous year. It was a casual arrangement, nothing serious, with no promises.

We were seven months in, and I'd let him slide through and break me off when I wasn't focused on school. Lincoln was the total package as far as I was concerned. He gave me everything I required. He was easy on the eyes, was a star basketball player, had a good head on his shoulders, a curve in his dick, and offered it up whenever I needed it.

"Hey, you," I answered with a smile as I flipped over onto my stomach.

His voice crackled through the line as he smirked. "Hey, yourself."

"What are you doing?"

I set the phone down on my nightstand before sliding off my wet panties and tossing them in the hamper. "Just finished an assignment for one of my classes."

"Word, how'd it go?"

"It's good, I think. I just hope my professor likes it. He's a bit of a hard ass when it comes to grading."

The word hard immediately made me wonder what Professor Hill was packing between his thighs. I'd seen his bulge against the fabric of his custom-fit trousers on more than one occasion and knew he had to be working with a monster.

"Why you got me lookin' at the ceiling?"

I picked up the phone and held it from the waist up. "I'm here. Happy now?"

"I was hitting you up because I just got out of practice, and I wanted to see if you wanted to grab somethin' to eat."

"Sick of the dining hall already, huh?" I joked.

"Hell yeah. I've been sick of that shit since my first year," he admitted.

I followed up with a quick chuckle before agreeing. "Food sounds good. Pick me up in thirty?"

Lincoln cleared his throat. "Cool, and while we eat, I'm hoping we can talk."

"About what?"

"About us, y'know, you and me."

"What about us?" I quizzed, sitting bare-assed on the edge of my bed.

"We've been kicking it for some time now, and I don't know about you, but I've been having a good time witchu."

I nodded in agreement. "I have too. I like what we have going on."

"I'm glad to hear you say that because I was hoping we could talk about taking things to the next level."

My lips twisted to the side. "And what level is that?"

"Being official. I want us to go public."

"Are you sayin' you wanna be my nigga, Lincoln Adams?" I queried with a slight giggle.

"Hell yeah, I wanna be your nigga, woman," he replied before belting out a quick laugh.

I sighed. "I mean, don't get me wrong, I'm flattered, but I thought when we started this, we both agreed on what it was. This *is* my last semester, Linc."

"I know, and I'm sayin' I wanna be more than that."

"I thought we were just having fun. I'm about to graduate soon, and—"

He sighed loudly into the receiver. "I know all of that. I just want you to know that I've been about yo' pretty ass for the past seven months, and I'm still about you."

I smirked. "Oh, really?"

"Yeah, and to show you how serious I am, we're having a little get-together this Friday night at my parents' house to celebrate my dad's birthday. It's nothin' big, just some family and friends. You should come through."

My brows hitched. "Oh shit, I'm meeting the fam now? You really must wanna wife a bitch up, huh?" I teased.

He sucked his teeth. "There your ass go playin' when I'm trying to be serious, woman."

I cheesed into the camera. "I'd be honored to meet your family. But listen, we've spent at least six of the thirty minutes I'm going to need to get ready to meet up with you, so I gotta go."

"Aight. I'll see you in a bit."

I quickly ended the FaceTime call and scurried to the bathroom for a quick shower. I couldn't believe I was entertaining the idea of being officially tied down to a junior, all while yearning for the touch of another man, a *grown-ass* man. A man I knew I'd probably never have but swore I would if I could.

———

Twenty minutes later, my phone buzzed with a text from Lincoln, letting me know he was downstairs. I delicately dusted my makeup brush down the bridge of my slender nose before moving to my prominent cheekbones. I quickly finished my look with a swipe of my favorite lip gloss against my pouty lips, giving it a shimmery sheen. I stood in front of the mirror with my scarf wrapped tightly around my neck and my honey-dipped melanated skin shielded under my favorite emerald green WBU Lions sweatshirt and peacoat. My almond-shaped eyes glinted with a hint of mystery. My wild, loose brown curls defied gravity most days and danced freely like leaves caught in a breeze. But I'd tamed my earthy brown strands with a beanie to cover my ears.

My cheeks flushed as I exited the dorm and descended the icy stairs.

Lincoln stood by the passenger side door with a smile on his face. His skin tone was a warm, inviting shade of light brown that carried a sun-kissed glow. The coils on top of his head stood tall and wild. His trendy high-top haircut added an edgy flair to his overall look. His brown orbs were deep and expressive, always sparkling with curiosity as if he were trying to read my thoughts. His stride was purposeful, and his smile was always genuine. Basketball stardom aside, people always gravitated toward him, sensing his approachability. Perhaps what I found to be his most attractive feature was the stubble that framed his jawline. It added a hint of rugged charm to his demeanor, making me clench my thighs together.

"Hey," I greeted him with a smile.

"Hey, gorgeous."

Lincoln laced his fingers with mine before pulling me into a warm bear hug. His familiar embrace held the promise of intimate secrets, shared meals, and laughs. He drove us to the cozy diner near campus, where neon signs, the smell of grilled cheese, and nostalgia awaited us. Inside, the air smelled of sizzling burgers and freshly brewed coffee. The bell above the door jingled as we walked in and settled into a cozy booth by the window. The moonlight spilled onto the red vinyl seats. At the counter was a mix of locals, students, and travelers watching the cook flipping pancakes on the griddle. It could be morning or midnight; the atmosphere never changed. The aroma created an appetizing medley, making my stomach growl. I glanced over the laminated menu offering various diner classics like juicy cheeseburgers, mozzarella sticks, and breakfast sandwiches.

"So, how was practice?" I inquired after the waitress took our orders.

"Tough. You know March Madness is around the corner, so the pressure's building up on and off the court. Coach is breathing down my neck. Every game feels like a fuckin' make-or-break moment. The fans, the scouts, everybody wants the best."

"Is basketball even still fun for you? Because from where I'm sitting, it sounds like you have the weight of the world on your shoulders, carrying the whole WBU team and all."

"I live for this shit, Ava."

I reached across the table to hold his hand. "I know you do. I just want you to learn to be gentle with yourself. Lincoln, you're incredible out there. Everybody knows that. But you're also human."

He scoffed. "Now you sound like my mother."

I shrugged. "I've never met the lady, but she sounds like a smart woman."

"Yeah. She is."

"Just remember, you're not alone. Win or lose, you still got me."

He squeezed my hand. "Thanks, but it's not just that. Jemal's been pushing me to skip practice and party all night."

I rolled my eyes. "I don't even know why you told me that. You know his ass is trouble. He's got a rap sheet longer than the Mississippi River, and he don't even go to our school anymore!"

"It's not his fault he lost his basketball scholarship freshman year."

"Mmm, yeah, right."

"He's my boy, Ava. We played ball on the same courts. It's hard to turn my back on him."

"All I'm saying is, if you follow his lead, you'll end up in a place you don't want to be. Loyalty is one thing, but survival is another."

"You right, and Coach won't tolerate any slip-ups."

"And neither will the streets," I added.

"Look at you talkin' to me all concerned and shit like you my girl," he teased.

I smirked while playfully fluttering my lashes toward the ceiling. "Whatever, boy. I'm just trying to look out for you."

"Well, speaking of you looking out for a nigga, there's something I've been thinking about. Something important."

My heart fluttered as Lincoln's words hung in the air. Suddenly, the cozy booth seemed to shrink, cocooning us in a private bubble.

"What is it?"

He took a deep breath. "You ain't give me a straight answer on the phone about us taking our relationship to the next level.

My mind raced. Going public meant stepping out of our secret haven, the late-night walks through The Yard, stolen kisses behind library shelves, and whispered confessions in my dorm room. It meant facing the world together, unfiltered.

"Lincoln, you know what that means, right? The media, your fans —they'll dissect every piece of our relationship. They'll want to know *everything*, and I don't get down like that. I don't like people in my business. I like how we are now. It's easy. It's simple."

He nodded. "I do. But I'm tired of hiding, Ava. Tired of pretending we're just friends who kick it from time to time. When I'm on the court, I want everyone to know who I got in my corner."

"And what if they judge us? What if—"

"Fuck them! They'll talk anyway. Let them. But I want to hold your hand in public, dance with you at parties, and celebrate my game victories together. I want the world to see us."

I swallowed hard. Somewhere along the line, the professor's handsome face faded into the backdrop of my mind, reducing him to a phantom of my creativity. I'd found solace sipping coffee with Lincoln, listening to his stories, offering genuine advice, and pretending that my intriguing forty-something-year-old professor didn't awaken my wildest desires. But going public with a star basketball player who was younger than me? Yikes. *Fuck. How the hell am I going to get out of this?*

THE STUDENT

It was six o'clock on the dot. I was in my usual seat diagonally across from the podium where Professor Hill typically began his lectures. As the class stretched on, he'd move about the room, talking with his hands as his lips moved in sync. As much as I adored his good looks and the intoxicating scent of warm vanilla musk that filled the room whenever he moved, he hadn't paid me any mind. He and his TA were extremely hard graders, one of the hardest I'd encountered since my calculus professor my sophomore year. And with graduation within reach, I couldn't afford to mess up. Since getting into Professor Hill's course, I couldn't begin to count the number of zeros, incompletes, and big fat F's I'd gotten because my poetry was considered *"too raunchy"* and didn't *"align with the assignment."* My latest poem, *Between My Thighs*, was no different. As witty as I thought I'd been with my words and alliterations, Professor Hill was far from impressed.

Professor Hill ended class after the first ninety minutes, which he'd never done before. He stood by the window, watching the delicate snowflakes dance outside as my classmates hurried to gather their belongings and vanish from the lecture hall before he changed his mind. I, on the other hand, took my time. I sat back and studied him. His milk chocolate skin was a rich tapestry of melanin. His stern yet handsome face was a testament to good genes, from his almond-shaped eyes to the gray dusting in his full beard. The inked tattoos against his exposed hands and forearms each chronicled a chapter of his mysterious life I'd love a sneak peek into. The classroom was almost empty before I started to gather my things. As soon as I got to my feet, I heard the professor call out to me.

"Miss Newman, may I have a word?" he requested, his voice measured.

I nodded as he stepped toward me before gesturing for me to sit. Professor Hill adjusted his tie before clearing his throat. "You're a talented writer," he said, choosing his words carefully. "But your latest assignment, it crossed a line."

My cheeks flushed. "I don't understand. It's erotic fiction. Creative writing. You didn't enjoy it?"

"I didn't say that," he admitted before letting out a long sigh. "Miss Newman, this was not the assignment that I gave you. I'm trying to work with you here, but I'm going to have to give you *another* zero," he explained.

"Why? It's part of the course," I interrupted. "We're supposed to explore taboo topics."

His patience waned as he leaned forward, palms flat on the desk. "Taboo, yes. But this? It's inappropriate."

"Well, can you at least give me some constructive criticism? Tell me what was wrong with *Between My Thighs*," I whined.

"Well, to be honest, your poem needs serious work."

"Weren't you the one who just called me a talented writer?"

"Yes, you have a way with words, Miss Newman, but it doesn't leave enough to the imagination. There's more to sex than the one-dimensional discussion of dick and pussy. Maybe if you paid more attention to the literature we discuss in class, you'd know that," he stated.

I frowned. "So you're saying my poem was one-dimensional? You tell me what's one-dimensional about the line: *sow your seeds across my field of jasmine and clover*. It's not like I said, *bust a nut all over me*. Pardon my French."

A huff of a laugh passed through his nostrils. "That's not the point. This is an exclusive course, Miss Newman. It's my job to push you to think deeper than genitalia. And it's your job to be able to do the work, especially if you want to graduate on time. Every week, we talk about erotic poetry from the Renaissance Era, right? So, show me *more* than the fucking. Show me its social, philosophical, or even political sides, too. You wanna pass my class? Then, just do the work I tell you to do how I tell you to, and make sure your participation in our class discussions is meaningful. It's that simple," he explained with a shrug. "Another slip-up could jeopardize your entire semester."

"Look, I'll do anything to get an A and pass this class. I can't afford to fail this close to graduation. I need these last three credits to graduate," I confessed.

Professor Hill's gaze bore into mine. "I'm sorry, but with all the incompletes, even if you ace everything else for the remainder of the semester, it's not likely that you'll walk out of here with anything higher than a low C," he confirmed.

I paced the room. "I won't accept a low C, Professor Hill. I can't. My scholarship, my future—"

He cut me off, silencing my spiral. "Your future isn't built on shock value, Miss Newman. You're giving away too much. You want to make the readers pause and hang on your every word. Simply put, make 'em work for it. That's all I'm saying."

My cheeks burned with embarrassment. "Is that what you've been doing to me?"

His brows rose toward his forehead. "Excuse me?"

"Making me work for it?" I asked while licking my lips and standing on my wedged heels.

"I'm not sure I follow."

"What do you want from me?" I sighed while twirling a loose ringlet of hair by my ear that dangled over my cartilage piercing. "Tell me what I can do, Professor Hill. I *need* to pass this class. I graduate in May. Is there any extra credit? Will you allow me to redo all the assignments I failed? Shit, I'll walk your dog if you want me to."

He let out another soft chuckle. "Look, I understand the pressure, but—"

My voice cracked. "No, you don't! You don't know what it's like. My parents... my family expects—"

He cut me off. "They expect nothing but greatness from you, right?" he challenged, finishing my sentence. "I get it. But this isn't the way."

"Then tell me what is," I suggested while propping myself up on the side of my desk.

Professor Hill cleared his throat as I slightly spread my legs, exposing the fact that I'd somehow managed to forget my panties. Clearly, he'd lost his train of thought somewhere between my left and right thigh. He folded his muscular arms across his chest and reeled back a few steps out of respect for my personal space.

"Miss Newman, I–"

"Please, call me Ava," I insisted in a honeyed tone.

"Ava," he replied sternly. "I'll allow you to revise your last two assignments. I want you to dig deeper. Explore eroticism without all the added sensationalism. Show me you've learned something beyond lewd composition."

My shoulders sagged before I widened my legs more. "And if I can't?"

"Then, we'll discuss the consequences."

"Which are?" I queried while standing up and closing the space between us.

"Miss Newman, I think you're charting dangerous waters."

I smirked, inching closer. "Dangerous, huh? Could you elaborate, Professor?"

"There's a thing called personal space, Miss Newman, and I happen to enjoy mine. Could you please back up?"

"Ava," I insisted before dropping my foot back a step.

"I think I've made it clear since the beginning of the semester that I'm interested in being more than your student, Professor Hill," I admitted. "And if I'm being honest, I didn't sign up for your class based on what you looked like, even though I know some did. I was genuinely interested in the topic of erotic poetry from the Harlem Renaissance era. It's just..."

"Not all you thought it'd be?" he questioned, finishing my sentence again.

I shook my head. "No, Professor Hill. It's *everything* I thought it would be and more."

"Then what's the issue?"

I flashed him a doe-eyed stare. "I didn't think it would be so hard to not fantasize about letting you fuck me all around this classroom."

My boldness made his eyes pop wide. "I'm flattered, Ava. But I must remind you that we're twenty years apart at best. I probably have shoes older than you in the back of my closet."

I flexed a half-shrug. "Doesn't change the fact that I want you."

He folded his arms across his bulging chest. "Humor me. What makes you want me? Because outside of these four walls, I'm willing to bet money you don't know shit about me," he confirmed.

"You're all I've thought about since the first night of your class. You challenge me in a way that no man my age ever could. I may be half your age, but trust me, Professor Hill, this baby don't cry."

I took my place a few inches away from him, cautioning before taking my next step. When he didn't move, I inched closer until I was close enough to touch him. My heart jumped against the reigns inside my chest as I reached out to slowly rub the inseam of his thigh.

"You're going to get me fired," he grumbled, succumbing to my gentle touch.

"Then tell your dick to stop poking my thigh," I insisted with a whisper.

"I can't do this. You're my student."

"Only for the next eight weeks."

"I'm married. I can't risk being seen with you here, not in this capacity," he explained as he rested his hand on my lower back.

I cupped his dick inside my hand, massaging his stiffness. "No one's here, Professor. Lock the door. You take care of me, and I'll take care of you. I promise I won't tell a soul."

THE PROFESSOR

Augustine Hill

My heart skipped a beat before I slowly removed her hand. It wasn't the first time a student had flirted with me, but Ava's aggressiveness caught me off guard. I pressed my lips together tightly as I gazed at the beautiful young woman before me. She was ripe and ready for the taking. It wasn't my first time noticing her sultry, deep coffee brown eyes or the way her warm vanilla skin tone and caramel apple brown lips looked as if they tasted as sweet as brown sugar. I admired the way her eyes sparkled with curiosity. She was the kind of student who lingered after class, asking questions that dove deeper than the syllabus. I noticed her from the beginning. It was hard not to. From how she leaned forward, pen poised, as if every word that fell off my tongue held the key to a hidden universe inside her. Whenever I lectured about erotic poetry, my gaze would always drift to her. She scribbled notes, her lips forming silent words. A part of me wondered if she knew how genuinely captivating she was—how her smile could light up even the darkest corridors and how her presence lingered long after she left the room.

In my many years of teaching, I'd never had a student be so assertive with me. Sure, some had tried, but it was nothing for me to use my wit to shut them down. But when it came to Ava Newman, nothing in me wanted to put up a fight. She wore her ebony black hair pulled up in a tight donut bun on the crown of her head with a few loose ringlets flying past her ears. I sank my teeth into my juicy bottom lip as my eyes shamelessly snaked from her cleavage to the short dress she wore that rode midway up her thighs whenever she crossed her legs. Jay-Z's five notorious words, *"Don't bite the apple, Eve,"* replayed in my head like a broken record, but the peach standing before me was too ripe not to taste.

It was my forty-second birthday, a milestone that had crept up like an unexpected gust of wind. For the first time, I felt the weight of those years—the accumulated wisdom, the hard lessons, the wins and losses. The thought that someone half my age was so intensely attracted to me was flattering, to say the least.

I cleared my throat, painfully aware of our age gap. "Ava, I appreciate your candor, and as tempted as I am, I can't. I'm—"

"You're married," she said, completing my sentence. "I know. Your wife, Dr. Cassandra Hill, is one of the school psychologists here, right? I've heard she's pretty brilliant."

My breath hitched. Cass—the queen who'd stood by me through the tumultuous years of academia. The one who understood my late-night grading sessions, my obsession with obscure Black poets, and how I sometimes lost myself in the labyrinth of words, amongst other things. She was my straight arrow in a crooked world.

"She's more than brilliant. She's my anchor," I responded softly.

Ava nodded. "I admire that... especially Black love and all, but I can't fight what I feel, Professor."

I chuckled. "Ah, the perils of being a middle-aged professor."

She smiled, revealing dimples that tugged at something deep within me. "But you wear it so damn well," Ava replied, eyeing my tailored suit pants.

I stroked my beard. "Thank you. I suppose I've earned a few of these gray hairs over the past forty-two years."

Ava's pools of brown twinkled as she stepped forward. She reached out to cup the side of my face. "Forty-two? You're aging like fine wine, Professor Hill. Besides, gray hairs can be quite distinguished, y'know."

"Thank you, and yeah, I turn forty-two today."

She smirked. "Really? Happy birthday, Professor."

I dipped my chin. "Appreciate it."

"I wish I'd known. I would've gotten you something."

I chuckled. "I already have everything I need, Ava, but thank you."

"Well, I hope you have a wonderful day. It's your birthday, after all. You deserve it."

I stepped over to lean against the podium, studying her. "You're a dangerous young woman, Miss Newman. I can see you getting me into a lot of trouble."

"Life's no fun without a little trouble, right?"

Ava dropped to her knees and proceeded to unbuckle my tailored trousers and briefs, freeing my semi-hard dick. She hungrily licked her lips before latching them around the tip and sucking it like a lollipop. I growled as she deep throated my dick. I knew she had a way with words, but her tongue was deadly. It made my toes curl in my designer loafers. I palmed the back of her head, gripping her bun.

"Mmm, shit. Show me how bad you want that A."

Her eyes sparkled with the promise of adventure as she slid her tongue up and down my shaft. "Mmm. I want it really bad, Professor."

"How bad?"

"Real bad." She panted before standing back up and bending over a nearby desk so that I could see her hairless pussy from behind.

My initial perception of her had been accurate. Ava Newman was a dangerous woman. She was a rogue with an appetite for mischief. She looked timid on the outside, but once you got her behind closed doors, she was a fuckin' savage in the sheets. Against my better judgment, my throbbing dick led me closer to her. We hadn't locked the door. We hadn't stepped away from the windows. And yet, the thrill of getting caught only made my dick harder. With her, I wanted to dance on the edge of legality, tiptoe across the boundary between right and wrong, and revel in the thrill of our forbidden acts. My curious fingertips skated up and down the back of her bare thighs before I gripped her plump ass and dipped inside her from behind.

"Oh shit," I growled. Ava's pussy was tight like a fist.

I pounded her pussy hard and fast as if I were going for broke. The harder I fucked her, the wetter she got. I reached around to grab her jiggling breasts, tugging on and flicking her nipples.

"Oooh shit! Yes, Professor Hill! Fuck this pussy!"

The thrill of it all was intoxicating. The adrenaline surged through my veins as I slipped in and out of her. But it wasn't just about the sex. Nah, it was the chase, the tantalizing terror of almost getting caught, that made me fuck her so good. The close calls were my aphrodisiac.

I pulled out of her long enough to spin her around and pick her up. She wrapped her legs around my waist as I pressed her back against the wall near the frosted windowpane.

"Ooh, yes. Yes, just like that," she purred as I fucked her slow and deep.

I growled against her neck, feeling the primal urge to give her the best dick she'd ever had. Her panting breath blew against my ear as she sucked on the diamond earring nestled in my right lobe.

Ava parted her lips and let the sweetest moan escape. "Mmm, let me ride it, Professor."

I kept her suspended in my grasp while taking her down to the floor. After a few deep strokes, I let her flip me over. Ava straddled my lap and eased onto me, engulfing me in her warmth. She moved like a goddess, her delicate fingers brushing against my lips—their stories whispering to my lips as I sucked on each one. Each thrust was a dance, a choreography of lust and desire. Her head dropped back as I sat up to suck on her hard, pierced nipples. Watching the desire expressed through her eye rolls and lip-biting was the sexiest shit I'd ever seen.

"I've never been this wet before, Professor," she confessed with a moan. "Touch it."

I reached down to massage her clit with my thumb. "Goddamn, that pussy is so wet. Oh, you must want that A real bad, don't you?" I challenged while gripping her throat and staring deep into her eyes.

"Mmm, so bad."

Ava continued to moan uncontrollably. They were the most delicate, sexy-sounding moans ever to bless my ears. Between the way she sounded and the feel of her pussy clenching my dick, I felt my nut surging from the soles of my feet.

"Oooh shit," I hissed. "I'm about to bust. Come catch this nut in your mouth."

She understood the assignment without question. She hopped off my lap, dropped between my legs, and spread her mouth wide. I stroked my shaft, while staring at her perky titties and long tongue anticipating the taste of my cream.

"Ooooh fuckkkkkkkk!" I groaned, spilling my seed into her warm, wet mouth.

Ava licked her lips after climbing back to a standing position and adjusting her clothes. "So, did I get it?"

I wiped the sheen of sweat from my brow and smiled. "Yes, Miss Newman, you got your A for this assignment, but I still expect your full potential in class. I won't be so lenient next time," I confirmed while zipping up my pants.

She smirked. "I'll remember that. But there may come a time when I'll need that extra credit opportunity again."

I toyed with the idea of splitting her from A to Z again, but before I could open my mouth to speak, my phone alarm sounded off with a reminder. "I'm sorry, but I have to go."

She nodded. "No worries, I can see myself out. Happy birthday again, Professor Hill," she replied, soft but confident.

"Thank you, Ava. Get home safe."

"You too."

———

The minute she reached the door, I heard the footsteps of students echoing down the marble corridor. We'd been close, so close, to getting caught. As she disappeared from my door, I knew she'd won. The thrill of the chase, the exclusive taste of my seed on her lips—it was all hers. I reveled in the satisfaction of having danced with danger herself, of being both the hunter and the prey. In my vacant classroom, secrets bloomed like forbidden flowers, and Ava Newman was their keeper. I knew better than anyone that secrets were the currency of life. And the one I shared with Ava was worth more than gold.

I trekked out of the ivy-covered university building, the cold sunset casting long shadows across the manicured lawn. I pulled out the keys in my coat pocket as I approached my sleek BMW. The phone in my pocket buzzed. I glanced at the screen. It was Vincent "Vinny" Russo, my business partner. Vinny was one of the only ones who knew the truth about my life, who I was, and the things I'd done to keep things quiet.

Mixed with Italian and African American blood, his glowing, olive skin had a relative brown hue. His hooked nose, dark curly hair, and excessive body hair came from his Italian roots, while his strong jawline, hazel eyes, and thick hair came from his African lineage.

"Brains," Vinny's gravelly voice crackled through the line. "Happy forty-second, my friend."

I leaned against the car, the weight of my secrets bearing down on me. "Thanks, Vinny. What's the occasion?"

"Good news," Vinny said. "The shipment's in. The merchandise is ready for distribution."

My heart rate didn't quicken. I didn't miss a step. The "merchandise" was a euphemism—the kind that danced on the edge of legality. I'd built an empire, not with textbooks and lecture notes, but with connections, wit, and a network that spanned the city of Potomac Falls' underbelly. To most, I was Professor Hill, the seasoned academic who dissected sonnets from the Harlem Renaissance era and debated the nuances of erotic literature. But to others, the ones who whispered in dimly lit bars and prison yards, I was Brains, a kingpin who held the city's fate in the palm of my hand. The nickname "Brains" had been bestowed upon me by the streets. It was a name that carried both respect and fear. Ever since I was young, my mind had been a steel trap, absorbing knowledge like a sponge, while my instincts kept me one step ahead of trouble.

"Where's the drop?" I quizzed, voice steady as I slid into the BMW. The leather seats were cool against my skin as I started the engine.

"Midnight," Vincent replied. "The old warehouse by the docks. You know the place."

I did. "Bet."

"Anything special planned for your birthday?" he inquired.

I glanced at the university clock tower as I drove by. I knew Cass was going to be at home waiting for me.

"Just a quiet dinner. Cass is making lasagna."

Vinny chuckled. "Domestic bliss, huh? You've got it all figured out."

"You already know what my plan is."

"Say less. Enjoy your night, my friend."

I disconnected the call, the weight of my choices settling on me like a cloak. Al Green's soulful voice filled the car, drowning out the distant hum of the city. As I drove through the winding roads toward my gated home in the hills, I found relief knowing I was almost done keeping up with the charade. My life as a seasoned academic at West Bridge University was merely a facade—a carefully constructed mask that concealed a darker reality. I'd been juggling the delicate balance of the ivory towers of academia and the murky alleys of the drug game for years. Behind closed doors, I orchestrated deals, laundered money, and ensured the flow of illicit goods. Every day, I stood at the crossroads of morality and temptation. The weight of my empire, the drug deals, and secret alliances weighed on my shoulders like an invisible cloak. But leaving it all behind? Could I sever the ties that bound me? The loyalty of the city's police, the money, the adrenaline of power? For years, it was a question that haunted me during the quiet hours of the night. Leaving meant gaining a newfound freedom.

I'd made it my goal to retire from it all, both the professor and the kingpin, for good at the end of the semester. The plan was to sell my house and move to the private beach house I'd purchased off the coast down south. Everything had an expiration date, and my time in the game was coming to an end on my terms. I'd paid my dues to the game.

I'd come a long way and damn sure didn't look like what I'd been through. I grew up in the crime-infested southside of Seven Pines. The overcrowded apartments were my home, and I quickly adapted to the harsh realities of survival in the streets. Trouble always had a way of finding me. By the time I was fourteen, I was already embroiled in a life of crime. Muggings, theft, and extortion were part of my repertoire. Shit, I even brought home my first gun at that age. The local gangs recognized my potential, and soon, I was running errands for the hustlers, delivering coded messages.

At sixteen, my path intersected with Vincent's. We ascended the criminal ladder together, navigating the gritty streets, building connections, and amassing influence. My brilliance was my armor, and I navigated the criminal underworld with finesse. Then came the turning point after high school. An encounter with a professor from West Bridge University opened a door I didn't know existed. Dr. Eric Sinclair saw past my tough exterior, recognizing my raw intelligence. He offered me a scholarship, more like a lifeline, to attend. I accepted, leaving behind the projects for the halls of academia. But I never severed my ties completely. The game had its hooks in me, and I straddled two worlds— the university and the streets. My students admired my intellect, unaware that I could also be their worst nightmare on any given day. Over the years, my leadership positioned me at the reigns of organized crime. The underworld trembled under my influence, and the Potomac Falls judicial system danced to my tune.

I drove through the gates and up the driveway, noticing the faint shadow of the moon hanging low over the mansion where I would celebrate my forty-second year. In truth, Vinny's good news was the best birthday present I could ask for. That, coupled with the thrill of danger and taste of forbidden fruit, was the beautiful Ava Newman. I stepped into my opulent home, where the hearty aroma of lasagna wafted past my nose. My beautiful wife awaited me in the kitchen, unaware of the smell of young pussy that clung to my tailored pants.

"Mmm. It smells good in here, baby," I told her.

I kissed her cheek, tasting the sweetness of her love, and wondered if redemption was possible for a man like me who loved straddling the line between peace and chaos.

Her full, inviting lips curved into a gentle smile. "I told you I was making your favorite, birthday boy."

"That's birthday *man* to you, woman. Let me get cleaned up for dinner. I'll be back down in a little."

"Okay, baby. And dress nicely. It *is* your birthday, handsome."

I kissed her forehead. "On it."

I was a lucky man. My wife was a goddess on earth. She carried herself with a level of grace unmatched by any other woman I'd ever encountered. Her complexion was a rich, velvety shade of brown, reminiscent of the finest milk chocolate. It glowed with the type of warmth and radiance only melanated skin could. Her hair cascaded in soft waves around her face, framing it elegantly. She'd cut her long hair bob length two years prior, and it only accentuated her beautiful features, the beach curls adding a touch of youthfulness. On her wrist was a delicate tattoo of a semicolon. It symbolized resilience, the continuation of a sentence when it could have ended. She wore it proudly as a daily reminder of the stories of countless lives she'd touched through her work as a psychiatrist. To her, every one of her patient's stories mattered.

Her chestnut brown eyes, deep pools of wisdom and empathy, sparkled when she looked at me. I didn't have to wear a mask with Cass. She knew about the coded messages, the hidden compartments, and the blood money that funded our lifestyle. But she *never* judged me for it. In her eyes, I was still the same man who'd been reciting poetry to her over breakfast for the past sixteen years, who kissed her forehead before leaving for the gym each morning. She believed in the goodness in me. I was simply the professor who molded young minds.

I proceeded down the hall and into my dimly lit study, where I traced the lines of a faded city map. It was the arteries of my underworld kingdom. I looked down at the city of Potomac Falls sprawled before me, its heartbeat echoing through the streets. I'd built my empire from the ground up, a house of cards stacked against the chaos. But with each passing year, the cards grew heavier, threatening to collapse. Nobody grew old in my profession, and I hadn't worked that hard not to be able to enjoy the fruits of my labor.

My thoughts of retirement from the game dissipated by the time I reached the master bathroom. The private space enveloped me in a cocoon of warmth and solitude as I stood naked at the fogged-over mirror. The steam from the shower curled around me like a sweet embrace.

I opened the frosted glass door and stepped inside. The warm and inviting water cascaded over my skin, washing away the day's sins. I adjusted the temperature, seeking the perfect balance between soothing and energizing. The soap smelled of eucalyptus, an aroma that eased the stress in my shoulders. But it wasn't just the physical fatigue that clung to me; it was the memory of Ava that occupied my thoughts.

She was unlike anyone I had ever known. Her spirit pranced with the grace of a little dove, fluttering free from the weight of the world. She was wild, untamed, and fiercely independent. Yet, there was a fragility about her that softened even the hardest parts of me. Her doe eyes were deep pools of mystery that reeled me in. Whenever she looked at me, and I mean really looked, I felt as if she could see the dark chapters of my humanity, and she wasn't the least bit afraid. But it was her lips that haunted me most, the way they curved into a sweet smile, the way her lip gloss tasted of summer strawberries. They were soft, inviting, and when she sucked me, they formed words that wrapped around my dick like a warm blanket. I imagined kissing those lips, tasting the sweetness of her moans.

As the water continued to pour down, I closed my eyes, picturing her beautiful face. Her hair, a wild tangle of chestnut waves, framed her face like a halo. I longed to bury my fingers in it again, to feel her curls against my skin. And her moan—the arousing sound of it echoed in my mind. It was infectious, like an erotic melody that played on repeat. The thought brought a smile to my face—a secret shared between only us two.

I stepped out of the shower, the steam dissipating, leaving me with a sense of shame for wanting to unravel the mystery behind her eyes and taste the sweetness of her lips again. I'd discovered something rare in Ava Newman. She was a young woman who was fierce, gentle, wild, and delicate. And I knew that if I could have her, even for a moment, I would change her life forever.

THE STUDENT

The water cascaded over my skin, washing away the professor's scent. I stood beneath the showerhead, eyes closed, as if the warm droplets could cleanse more than just my body. The rest of my night was supposed to be simple: a polite dinner with Lincoln at his parents' house. But as the water swirled down the drain, so did my resolve.

"Tell him you're not coming," my reflection whispered. *"You're tired, and it's not like it's his birthday. You don't even know his damn parents."*

But Lincoln had gone out of his way to invite me. He'd been texting me all day, telling me how eager his family was to meet me. I sighed. I wasn't heartless. I couldn't be a buzzkill and cancel at the last minute. Besides, Lincoln was sweet, a little too sweet, perhaps. His family, though, was a mystery. I'd never met them, and the thought of mingling with strangers made my stomach churn.

I stepped out of the shower, wrapping my body in a plush towel. I gently slid my finger across my exposed collarbone as flashbacks of my time fucking Professor Hill replayed in my mind. Being with Professor Hill was everything I thought it would be. The dick was better than Chick-Fil-A on a Sunday. Before I got too wrapped up in my daydreams, I noticed my reflection staring back at me.

"Get dressed and go," it urged. *"Smile, nod, eat cake, and leave. No harm, no foul."* By the time I decided what to wear and got dressed, Lincoln had sent a text with the address.

"Ten-seven-thirty-five Grasswood Terrace," I mumbled while typing the address into my GPS.

Dressed in a simple black dress and knee-high boots, I climbed into my car. The GPS guided me through winding streets, past manicured lawns and imposing gates. I'd never been to that part of the city before. The neighborhood was a world apart from my modest dorm. *"Too rich for my blood,"* I muttered, gripping the steering wheel of my used Toyota Corolla.

My breath hitched when I pulled up to the grand house nestled among the tall oaks. The mansion stood firm, its dozens of windows gleaming. Lincoln appeared at the door just as I approached it.

His face was alight with joy. "Ava!" he exclaimed before pulling me into a hug. "I'm glad you made it!"

"Of course," I replied, my voice steadier than I felt.

He led me through the grand foyer, past crystal chandeliers and marble floors. The air smelled of money—polished wood, expensive perfume, and mystery. The screened-in porch awaited, its long table adorned with sparkling silverware that could feed a small village. And there, at the head of the table, sat renowned Professor Augustine Hill. His salt-and-pepper beard framed a stern face, and his seductive brown eyes bore into my soul. Out of all the things I could've expected, I never expected this. The man who'd lectured and licked me was hosting me for dinner. I wasn't in just any house. *I was in Professor Hill's home.* Before either of us could speak, Lincoln introduced me.

"Ava, I want you to meet my mom and dad, Cassandra and Augustine Hill–"

"Professor Hill?" I quizzed, cutting him off as my brow caved in.

"Yup. This is my stepdad, Professor Augustine Hill. Mom, Dad, I want you to officially meet my girlfriend, Ava Newman."

"Ava," Professor Hill acknowledged, rising from his seat. The way my name fell off his tongue made me wet. He extended his hand to mine. His handshake was firm, his gaze assessing as if he hadn't seen my

unmentionables a few hours prior. "We finally meet the beautiful wraith. My son speaks highly of you. A brilliant mind, he says."

I cleared my throat. "T-thank you, Professor," I stammered as my mind raced. "It's a pleasure to be in your home."

"Please, call me Augustine."

He gestured for us to take our seats at the table. "Dinner is almost ready. We prefer al fresco dining."

I followed behind Lincoln like a lost puppy, my heart pounding. The porch overlooked a moonlit garden, its blooms swaying in the chilling night breeze. The table was set with fine China. A regal woman with pearls and a warm smile appeared. She couldn't have been anyone other than Lincoln's mother.

"Ava, we're delighted to finally meet you."

"Likewise," I replied, mind whirling as if stuck on a merry-go-round. "Your home is beautiful."

"Thank you. With a few upgrades, you'd never be able to tell it's been in the family for generations," she shared. "Overall, it's been Augustine's academic research that's funded our lifestyle."

I glanced at Lincoln. He was oblivious, chatting with his father about something. But my eyes met Professor Hill's, and in that moment, I understood. The wealth and mystique all traced back to him. And me? I just happened to be the outsider who'd stumbled into their wealthy world.

"Before we sit for dinner, do you wanna take a quick tour?" Lincoln suggested.

I nodded, thankful for the opportunity to get out of Augustine's sight line. "I'd like that. But, uh, can I use your bathroom first?"

Lincoln lovingly laced his fingers with mine. "Sure. It's this way."

He led me to the powder room down the hall and waited for me on the other side of the door. "I'll only be a second," I promised before closing the door.

Professor Hill's powder room was a sanctuary of marble and muted elegance. The scent of lavender hung in the air, soothing yet tinged with luxury. I stood before the gold-trimmed mirror, my reflection wavering. The professor's home, his intimate space, had reeled me in like a moth to a forbidden flame. I'd never been in a recluse's home before, especially not one who lectured on erotic literature by day and hid behind thick oak doors by night.

Seeing him again and meeting Lincoln's mother for the first time made my pulse race. I'd contemplated faking an illness and fleeing before dinner started, but my curiosity held me captive.

"Tell Linc you're sick," my inner voice urged. *"Get out before shit gets even more weird."*

But the secrets lining the walls of the professor's home whispered to me as I succumbed to the thrill of his unknown world. I turned on the sink and flicked a few water droplets against my face before drying my hands and walking out.

"Ready?" Lincoln asked.

"Ready," I confirmed.

Lincoln led me through the abundant space, past crystal chandeliers in each room and the sweeping staircase in the foyer.

"It's breathtaking, but how do they afford all this?" I whispered. "Both of them work at the university, right?"

Lincoln chuckled. "My mom told you it's been in the family for generations."

"Yeah, but this looks like more than old money. This place is practically a mini castle."

"You don't get out much, do you?"

"I won't lie. I've been in Potomac Falls for four years, and I've never been on this side of town before."

He grinned. "Well, my dad is a renowned professor, and my mom is a doctor. It's nothing out of the ordinary. He's worked hard and invested wisely. But he doesn't flaunt it."

"So, what you're saying is there's no more to the story."

He shrugged. "Nah."

"I can't lie. It would've been nice to know you've been hiding a secret weapon all this time."

He raised an eyebrow. "Secret weapon? What are you talking about?"

"Your stepdad, Professor Hill. When you said I'd be coming for your stepfather's birthday, I didn't expect it to be him."

"Yeah. He's been around since I was four. He's really the only father I've ever known."

"What happened to your biological father?"

"Prison doing a fifty-year bid."

"Damn. I'm sorry."

"It's cool. I'm better off with who I have as a dad now. Besides, I never knew the nigga. You can't miss a relationship you never had. The only thing I got from his ass was his last name."

"Wow. I still can't believe the one who wields the power of grades like a wizard with a wand has raised you since you were practically a toddler. This is the smallest world ever."

"Yeah, well, I don't make a big deal out of it because I don't want to be hounded by the endless females trying to get into his class each semester. Believe it or not, that nigga is sort of a sex symbol around campus."

I huffed. "Oh yeah?"

"Yeah. That's why I never changed my last name to Hill, like everyone expected. I like being separate from my parents' legacy—their shadow. I wanted to carve my path at West Bridge and build my reputation, especially playing basketball. I didn't want people to think I got my spot on the team based on who my parents were."

I dipped my chin. "Nobody wants to live in someone else's shadow forever. I get it. Your secret is safe with me. But had I known you had my professor in your back pocket, I would've had you whispering in his ear about my grade since the start of the semester."

His brow lurched toward his crisp hairline. "Are you flunking his class or something?"

I rolled my eyes. "No, not flunking. But I don't think he or his TA appreciate my taste in poetry. Apparently, they're not fans of haikus about the female genitalia."

A surge of laughter burst past Lincoln's lips as his eyes crinkled at the sides. "Yo, you're wild as hell, girl." He stopped in his tracks and turned to me. "Thank you for coming out tonight."

"I promised I would, and a promise is a promise."

"I know we've been playing things fast and loose for the past few months, but now that you've officially met my parents, I want an answer about going public."

"Lincoln, we talked about this a few nights ago…"

"Yeah, and you never really gave me a straight answer."

"You kinda already introduced me to the parentals as your girl, so…"

He smirked. "I did, huh?"

A soft laugh escaped my lips. "Yeah. You did."

"So, you good with that or…"

I shot him an apprehensive look. "Lincoln, I'm a senior, and you're a junior. We're on different paths."

"I don't care about paths, Ava. I care about us."

He'd made it painfully clear he wanted more than late-night coffee, study dates, and stolen kisses in the dorms. I didn't want to break his heart. I couldn't. Graduation was only a few months away. All I had to do was hold on until then. *Stick with him until after graduation. That's the plan, Ava.*

I eased out a steady breath. "Okay, then. I guess we're doing this."

"Yeah?" he queried, brows high with anticipation.

I nodded. "Yeah."

Lincoln leaned in, capturing my lips in a soft kiss. It was sweet, uncertain, and filled with unspoken promises. Just then, his mother's voice echoed down the hall. "Lincoln, Ava, dinner's ready!"

We broke apart when we heard his mother's heels clicking against the marble floor. She was a vision in silk and pearls, her eyes assessing me more than him. Lincoln and I met her halfway before she spoke up again.

"Linc, can you help your father outside? He's having trouble with the patio heaters."

"Sure."

"Ava and I will be right along."

Lincoln nodded. "Okay."

"My son adores you," Lincoln's mother told me when he was out of earshot. "He's always been soft-hearted."

I glanced at the woman's perfectly manicured nails before flashing her a warm smile. "He's wonderful," I replied. "And your home, it's exquisite."

"Thank you," she responded as her eyes narrowed. "You're different," Mrs. Hill acknowledged as we walked. "Not like the others he's brought home."

My throat tightened. "Different how?"

Her knowing gaze bore into her. "You're curious. I can tell you look at our world as if it's some sort of puzzle. But beware, my dear. Puzzles have missing pieces."

Her statement boggled my mind. Was her cryptic message a warning? Or a test? I'd danced with danger before, but for the first time, I was waltzing with the professor's wife. *You just have to get to the cake, and you can leave,* I reminded myself while trying to play it cool. Secrets had a way of unraveling, and being in Professor Hill's home hours after I'd fucked him made me realize I'd stepped into a web of them.

———

The dinner unfolded like a carefully choreographed ballet. I balanced my plate, engaging in small talk with Lincoln's mother. The warm patio heater next to me hummed with the clink of silverware and the murmur of cultured voices. Professor Hill sat at the head of the table, his gaze occasionally flickering toward mine. I was no longer just his student but an intruder in his world.

Lincoln leaned in and whispered, "Isn't this amazing? My father's connections run deep."

I nodded, my fork tracing patterns on my dinner plate. "Indeed," I replied, voice steady as if I hadn't been zoning out to my thoughts. "Your family history is fascinating."

As the evening wore on, my pasted-on smile became a mask. I listened to stories of philanthropy, Black art acquisitions, and prestigious galas. My heart rate quickened when dessert arrived, a decadent red velvet birthday cake. I was almost at the finish line.

Lincoln's mother, elegant and poised, joined the conversation. "Everyone, let's sing Happy Birthday."

The three of us stood around and sang happy birthday to Augustine before watching him blow out his candles and cut the cake.

"I hope you saved room for dessert, Ava," his mother commented before serving me a slice of cake.

Little did she know, my sweet tooth had been satisfied hours prior when I'd been licking her husband's lollipop. The red velvet birthday cake sat untouched on my plate; its sweetness tasted bitter. I knew it was nothing but my guilt. I'd danced with danger, and now I had to face the aftermath.

The Wife

Cassandra Hill

I sat across from my husband of sixteen years with my gaze fixed on him. He wore his age well for it to be his forty-second birthday. I'd seen plenty of men hit their genetic demise long before then and was grateful I still had a man who looked good enough to eat. I'd meticulously planned Augustine's birthday dinner, hoping to rekindle the spark that had flickered in our marriage almost two decades prior. His salt-and-pepper beard was neatly combed, and the candlelight danced in his eyes as he leaned forward to blow out the single candle on his dessert. My heart swelled with affection. I remembered the early days, our stolen kisses, late-night conversations, and shared dreams. But lately, something had changed. I could see it in his face.

The calls on my phone had been relentless for hours, and I knew they weren't from work or family. My phone vibrated again as Augustine cut into his slice of red velvet cake. Unable to take it any longer, I excused myself, slipping away from the table. In the dimly lit corridor, I pulled out my phone, the screen illuminating my worried expression. The caller I.D. showed a familiar name and number. It was the same one that had haunted my dreams, the one I'd traced to a late-night rendezvous at private hotels. My fingers trembled as I typed a message to my husband's teaching assistant, Karina.

Me: *Can't talk now.*

Karina: *Meet me at the usual spot. Urgent. I think he's cheating again.*

Me: *Okay.*

My trembling fingers pressed send as my heart plummeted to my soles. I'd confronted Augustine about his affairs in the past, but he had always denied them, promising to change. Yet there I was, caught in the same web of suspicion and betrayal. I leaned against the cold wall, mind racing with questions. *Is it another student? A colleague? Or, worse, someone I know?*

I shook it off and masked myself with my game face before returning to the party with a strained smile. Back at the table, Augustine sipped his wine, oblivious to the turmoil unfolding just outside. I would play the part of the doting, loving wife celebrating her husband's birthday, but tomorrow, I'd get to the bottom of things. The truth would surface, and our marriage would either continue to crumble at the foundation or find a way to heal.

I raised my glass in my husband's honor, my fingers brushing against the cool crystal. "Happy birthday, baby," I whispered as my eyes searched his face for any sign of guilt.

But he only smiled, blissfully unaware of the storm brewing in the pit of my stomach. At that moment, I vowed to uncover the truth. His affair, real or imagined, would no longer remain hidden in the shadows. I would meet Karina and face the truth, even if it shattered my heart. Then, I would decide whether to fight for our love or let it slip through my fingers like sand.

———

I was first introduced to the drug game through my first husband and Lincoln's biological father, Marcus. He had eyes dark as storm clouds and a temper to match. Marcus liked his money like he liked his women, fast. Unfortunately, I didn't find that out until I was already three months pregnant with our son and head over heels in love. Marcus taught me the ins and outs of the game. He had ambition. He just lacked the ability to hold down the position at the top before the Feds swooped in and took everything. They left my son and me without a pot to piss in and hauled him off to do a fifty-year bid, practically a lifetime behind bars.

My entire world ended after the courtroom whispered the guilty verdict. Lincoln was only a mere toddler then, clinging to my leg. His innocence was a fragile shield against our new harsh reality. Lincoln was the thread that bound me to both sorrow and recovery. I worked two jobs, my hands calloused from scrubbing floors, writing papers, and wiping tears. The prison visits were a ritual, Lincoln pressing his small palms against the cold glass, his father on the other side, staring back at us through hollow eyes. After a year of that, I served him divorce papers like a final plea for freedom. He knew our love had unraveled, frayed by betrayal and violence.

I navigated single motherhood for the next year and a half, my heart broken beyond repair. Until, one autumn afternoon, fate intervened. Augustine, the handsome stranger with kind eyes and a gentle smile, crossed my path. He had no children of his own, but he carried an innate tenderness, the kind that could heal wounds and fix broken hearts. We met at a community center where Lincoln attended a daycare program. Augustine volunteered there, his laughter mingling with the children.

He taught Lincoln how to ride a bike at five. He listened to my origin story and secrets I dared not share with anyone else. His gentle but firm touch was the opposite of Marcus's bruising grip. And when he held Lincoln, my son's eyes widened as if recognizing a missing piece of his puzzle since his father had been incarcerated. I resisted at first, naturally fighting the pull of attraction and the vulnerability that came with opening up to someone after being hurt. But he persisted. Augustine cooked dinners, helped with homework, and tucked my son into bed so well that he hardly ever got up in the middle of the night. The three of us became a family. Once I informed him of my ex's situation, he never asked about him again.

As seasons changed, so did our bond. He became Lincoln's confidant, who listened to all of his schoolyard woes and girl troubles. He taught him to tie a tie, throw a baseball, and believe in second chances. And when Lincoln called him *Dad* for the first time, my heart swelled. It was a title earned not by blood but by choice. Marcus remained a distant figure, a phantom in Lincoln's sleepy-eyed questions before bedtime. The letters from prison arrived sporadically, filled with remorse and promises of change. But I'd moved forward for the better, my love redefined by Augustine's unwavering masculine presence in our lives.

So, when Augustine came to me the night before our wedding and told me about his involvement in the drug game and the empire he'd built from the ground up, I didn't bat an eye. Augustine was everything Marcus could never be. He was a real boss and commanded his full respect whenever he entered a room. I couldn't have been prouder to become his wife. We married quietly, our vows whispered under blooming cherry blossoms in a secret garden. Lincoln stood between us, a testament to resilience. He shed his double life, and I became his anchor. The stacks of random cash and coded messages meant nothing to me. He was simply Augustine, the man who loved me fiercely, whispered poetry against the crevices of my brown skin, and looked at my son as his own.

As the years unfolded, responsibilities settled upon our shoulders. I pursued my career as a psychologist and landed a job at the university while Augustine immersed himself in academia, teaching taboo literature to eager minds. Our home echoed with laughter, arguments, and whispered apologies as we navigated the delicate balance of shared dreams and individual aspirations. But lately, cracks had appeared. His late nights at the university, the mysterious phone calls, and the scent of mall kiosk perfume lingering on his clothes, all whispered secrets that gnawed at my heart.

I wondered if our love could withstand betrayal if the promises we made under those cherry blossoms still held weight. I wondered if he remembered the first time he knew he'd fallen in love with me. Could he still feel the rhythm of our love? Could I? Both men, the one who had shattered my heart and the one who had stitched it back together, had taught me valuable lessons. And over the years, I'd learned to keep quiet and get my wins in silence.

———

My phone vibrated with another text from Karina, drawing me back to the present.

Karina: *I hope you're not over there spiraling. We both know you deserve better. I love you.*

I sighed, leaving the message on read before locking the phone. Karina Ahmed was a beautiful young woman of Eritrean descent. Her smooth complexion was like warm honey under the morning sun. A dark pixie cut framed her face, revealing the elegant curve of her neck. Whenever she ran her fingers through it, I'd find myself smiling in approval. Her glasses were always both practical and stylish, adding an intellectual allure as they sat perched on the bridge of her slender nose. Her sensual lips curved like the crescent moon, inviting me to spill my secrets. Karina's deep-set brown eyes were the portals to her soul. I'd always been secretly jealous of her naturally long eyelashes. They were like delicate fans, casting shadows on her cheeks whenever she blinked.

She became a patient of mine during her sophomore year, when her father's terminal illness had cast a shadow over her life, a relentless storm that threatened to drown her in grief. She found solace under my care. Aside from her beauty, it didn't take me long to become dazzled by her brilliant mind. At the end of her junior year, I recommended her for my husband's TA position. Her vibrant personality won over Augustine, and she became the new teaching assistant for his erotic poetry class. Karina was a quiet presence. Her eyes held secrets, and her soft hands carried the weight of countless essays. I'd seen her struggle, the mascara-streaked cheeks, the sleepless nights, the fragile smile she wore like armor. And so, she lingered after her sessions, offering me a cup of luke-warm coffee and a listening ear.

Our conversations outside of her sessions began innocently, an analysis of erotic sonnets, conversations about debates she'd had with Augustine about metaphors, and our shared love for dusty bookshops. But beneath the academic veneer, something deeper stirred. I found myself confiding in her. Karina listened, her doe-eyed gaze unwavering as if she were hanging on to my every word. She became my sounding board, the one who understood my needs without judgment.

When her father's health deteriorated further, she crumbled. She wept in my arms. My embrace was sanctuary and sin—the abyss of desire threatened to swallow us whole. Our bodies danced on the edge between patient and healer, between forbidden and necessary. She sat by his hospital bedside, watching his life slip away like sand through her fingers. I held her hand and whispered words of comfort when her world blurred into gray. We met three times a week until I nursed her back to health, both professionally and personally.

Our relationship blurred boundaries. Our stolen glances became the brush of her sweet fingertips against my clit, and the unspoken promises whispered against my folds. Late nights in my office turned into whispered erotic confessions—the feel of her breasts, the fragility of her lips against mine. My touch was unprofessional and carnal, eyes displaying a longing that mirrored hers.

With the help of her younger brother, Karina nursed her father back to health, but it was my pussy that healed her fractured spirit. It wasn't until she told me what my husband's students whispered about him and other women on campus. She was my mole and my dirty little secret. She scratched my back, and I scratched hers. My relationship with Karina had remained a secret, a whispered confession in the private walls of my office or the confinement of hotel rooms. I wore my wedding ring, but it was Karina's tongue game that had me hooked. The way she had my toes throwing up gang signs on my office chaise should've been illegal. It probably was based on our professional relationship alone. Yet, I'd allowed it to continue for the better part of a year.

I knew I needed to end our personal relationship. The words hovered on my lips, a confession waiting to break free. But each time I considered it, I saw her smile, her brown eyes crinkle, the warmth that radiated between my thighs from her feminine touch. She deserved more than what I could give her. I loved my husband and had no plans to leave him for a woman half my age. She didn't deserve to be pacified with the safety of ignorance. She'd already been through too much.

The Professor

When Ava left, I felt like I could finally settle my nerves. It had been hard to breathe the entire time she'd been in my presence. Lincoln swaggered back into the kitchen after walking her out to her car. His mother and I were in the kitchen scraping leftovers off the dirty dinner plates before placing them in the dishwasher.

"So, son, tell me about your new girlfriend," I said casually.

Lincoln was so smitten with her that he couldn't help but smile. "Yeah. She's amazing, Dad. Smart, funny, and beautiful. We've been kicking it for a few months and decided to make things official."

"And how did you two meet? I never did get to ask that," Cass interjected.

"At a party off campus. It turned out she was actually in one of my classes. I know, I know, it's a bit unconventional, but we clicked instantly."

Cass nodded. "Interesting. What does she study?"

"She's a communications major. This is her last year at West Bridge. She's in your class, right, Dad?" Lincoln questioned.

I cleared my throat. "Yes, Miss Newman is a student of mine."

Cass shot me a narrowed glare before turning her attention back to Lincoln. "I can tell you really like her. But, baby, you know relationships can be complicated, especially when a slight age gap is involved. I mean, have you discussed what will happen after she graduates?"

"I'm not a baby, Mama. I know what I'm doing with Ava. I wouldn't have brought her around if I didn't. She's not like any other girl I've ever been with," he confessed.

I sighed. "You don't want to hear it, but your mother is right. I've seen many students fall in love during their college years. Sometimes, it's genuine. Other times, it's... complicated," I added.

"What is up with you two? Ava and I are adults. We're both consenting—"

Cass waved her hand to stop him. "Of course you are. But emotions can blur lines, Lincoln. And sometimes, they can lead us down unexpected paths. I don't want to see you get your heart broken."

Lincoln squinted his chestnut-colored eyes. "Why are you two so concerned about my relationship with Ava? You've never been this interested in my other girlfriends before."

"We're your parents. It's our job to be concerned about the people you bring into our lives," I explained. "I don't know why you're acting as if we haven't had this conversation in the past."

"So, what? You want me to break up with her?" he asked defensively.

"No, no. We're not saying that. We're just saying be careful, that's all," Cass answered, smoothing things over as only she could.

Lincoln sighed. "Fine, yeah. I'll be careful. But I'm telling y'all, Ava is the real deal. Even if she knew about what our family was into, I think she'd be cool with it."

"You think, or you know?" I quizzed, hoping my question would make him see the flaws in his thought process.

"It's not like we've talked about it, but it's a feeling I have."

I swung my head in a no. "She's not family, Lincoln. I know her young pussy got your nose wide open, but don't you *ever* forget that. *We* are your family. Your loyalty lies with us. Do you understand that?"

Lincoln sighed. "Yes. I understand."

"Good. Now finish helping your mother with the dishes and meet me in my study. I have some business to discuss with you," I stated before exiting.

I'd only brought up Ava to gauge how my son felt about her so that I could determine how I'd move when it came to her in the future. She was bright, yes, but there was something more. Something about her tugged at something deep inside me. I'd watched her grow, seen her passion ignite. And now that I'd felt her, seeing her sitting in my class, unaware of my urge to fuck the shit out of her because of my son's feelings, would be a constant battle. Truthfully, I *enjoyed* fucking Ava, and as much as I wasn't trying to have *any* drama at my age, I would be lying to myself if I said I didn't want the chance to slip and slide inside her again.

———

I looked around my cozy study lined with mahogany bookshelves and the crackling fireplace. The room smelled of aged leather and wisdom as I paced the imported Persian rug with my phone clutched as Vincent explained the bad news.

"*What*? How could this happen? I thought you said everything was fine with the shipment!" I paused when I heard a knock on the door. "Fine, I'll handle it."

Lincoln sailed inside and sat on the edge of my grand mahogany desk. "You wanted to see me?"

I eyed him closely. "Son, you know I've always been honest with you, right?"

He nodded. "Yeah, Dad. What's going on? What's wrong?" he probed, voice laced with concern.

"Something went down with one of my... business arrangements. I need you to make a run for me. It's urgent."

His eyebrow raised in curiosity. "What kind of run?"

I looked away. "It's crucial, Lincoln. I'm asking you because I trust you. You're *my* son."

Lincoln leaned forward. "Dad, you're scaring me. What's really going on?"

"You just stood in my face in the kitchen and told me you were a man, right? So, I need you to do this for me tonight. No questions asked."

"Tell me what it is, and I'll do it."

I sighed. "Meet your Uncle Vinny at the old warehouse by the docks and get in the van. Drive it to the address I send you. No delays, no hesitations. Can I count on you?"

My instructions to Lincoln were cryptic, revealing nothing beyond urgency and trust.

"Of course, Dad. But—"

"Good. Now, about your twenty-first birthday next week. What are your plans?"

His demeanor brightened. "I was going to ask Ava to join me at our family's private beach house for spring break. I wanted to show her where we spent summers as a kid."

I thought we'd been done speaking about her, but it was clear she ran through his mind twenty-four-seven. Whenever she entered my thoughts, the phrase *wetter than water* came to mind. "She's important to you, isn't she?" I quizzed.

He smiled wide. "Yeah, she's amazing. I've never felt this way before."

I dipped my chin. "I can tell."

"What makes you say that?"

"Because each time you speak about her, I can tell you're letting her into our lives more and more."

"I'm telling you, she's the real deal. She's solid. She can handle the pressure of being a part of our family. Besides, all this will be mine to run one day, right?"

My brows creased. "What makes you think that?"

"Listen, Dad, I know you want to retire, and I'm only a year away from graduating. I'm ready for more responsibility outside of basketball."

I wagged my head from left to right. "You're not ready, Lincoln. And even if you were, you need to focus on basketball."

He huffed, frustrated. "You made me promise you I'd get my education first, and I'm doing that, but I can do more," he offered eagerly. "I'll learn the game. I'll—"

I folded my body into the armchair and clasped my hands. "No, Lincoln. I've made my choice. All I need you to do is make the drop. Trust me, it's better this way. You're not ready for this life."

"Why do you keep saying that shit, Dad?"

I sighed. I loved my son, but he was too soft for the harsh realities of the game. The only game he needed to be focused on was the one on the court. But if he wanted to be treated like a man, I would do just that and give the truth to him straight, no chaser.

"Because you see the world through rose-tinted glasses. You believe in kindness, fairness, and the goodness of people. You get it from your mother, and that's beautiful, my son. Your compassion and empathy are rare gems in this cutthroat world. But the game don't give a fuck about compassion. It's not a fairy tale. It's a battlefield. It chews up the soft-hearted and spits them out."

Lincoln lowered his gaze. "So, what are you saying?"

"When I retire, I'm handing over everything to Vinny to let him run things how he wants. He's grizzled, battle-scarred. He can stomach the blood and make heartless decisions. He knows how to navigate these treacherous waters of the game. He's the captain this ship needs."

"But I thought—"

I cut him off. "You thought sentimentality would sway me? Lincoln, there is no love in the game. It doesn't keep the enemies off your back or keep you safe at night. Vinny has earned this. He's bled for this. And he'll continue to steer things toward prosperity long after I'm gone."

"And what about me?"

"You'll find your own path. Maybe it's running your own I.T. company, painting sunsets, or writing poetry. But it won't be here, in my ruthless arena."

"I just don't want to disappoint you."

"You won't if you continue to play your role, son."

He sighed, looking defeated. "Okay, I got you."

———

After class that following Friday, while all my other students hurried out of the lecture hall, Ava lingered by the window, the campus lights casting shadows on her face. I cleared my throat while leaning against the podium.

"So, Miss Newman, my son mentioned you're his girlfriend."

She blinked rapidly for a couple of seconds. "It was news to me too. We've been... seeing each other. But labels and unwanted publicity? It's not really my thing."

"Does he know that?"

She sighed, lean shoulders sagging. "He's sweet, and I don't want to hurt him."

I raised an eyebrow. "How long has this been a thing?"

Ava shrugged. "About eight months or so. At first, things were casual, and then he said he wanted to get more serious and take things public."

"Mmm. I see. He said you two are visiting our beach house to celebrate his birthday this weekend."

She nodded. "Yeah. When he mentioned the beach house, I couldn't get the picture of waves out of my head. I'm eager to escape the city for a while and clear all this haze from my mind."

"It's one of my favorite places to go when I need to do just that. I'm sure the waves will give you all the clarity you need, Little Dove."

She blinked, caught off guard. "What?"

A chuckle slipped from my lips when her confusion made me realize I may have overstepped. "I apologize," I replied quickly. "I shouldn't have said that out loud."

Her cheeks flushed as she tucked a stray curl behind her ear, a habit she had when she was nervous. "I've never been called that before, but I like it," she admitted with a warm smile. "No need to apologize."

"Thank you."

"No problem."

"I'm sure you already know this, but it's Lincoln's twenty-first birthday. Please don't let him get too wasted, okay?"

Ava chuckled. "Don't worry, I won't."

She turned to walk away, and I expelled an audible sigh. "Ava, wait."

"Yes, Professor Hill?"

"You do understand that in my position I *don't* do drama, right?"

"No drama, I promise," she replied, holding up her first three fingers. "Scout's honor."

"Good. My home is my sanctuary. It has always been drama-free. Until now."

"Trust me, Professor, I had no idea you and Lincoln were... Listen, I respect boundaries. I promise I won't bring chaos into your home."

I leaned in closer to her. "You're an impressive woman, Ava. You sat at the same table with me and didn't blow my cover or yours. But secrets have a way of unraveling."

She smirked. "I won't tell if you won't."

I studied her beautiful features while fighting the burning desire to touch her again. But I knew better. She was already too close to home.

"Be safe this weekend and enjoy yourself, Miss Newman."

"Thanks, Professor."

The Stepson

Lincoln Adams

I woke up on my twenty-first birthday with a sense of anticipation. The sun peeked through the curtains, glowing warmly on the posters that adorned my dorm room walls. The day when I would finally step into adulthood had finally arrived. I swung my legs over the edge of the bed, feeling the cool wooden floor beneath my feet. My heart raced as I imagined buying out the liquor store a few blocks off campus. For years, I'd watched others buy alcohol with envy. Now, it was my turn. I could walk in, pick out a bottle, and flash my legal ID with pride—no more sidelong glances or awkward explanations. But there was more to my special day than just alcohol. My parents still saw me as their little boy, even though I'd long outgrown my childhood basketball sneakers. If it wasn't about basketball, they hovered, worried about my every move, oblivious to the secret I'd been harboring.

Six months ago, I received a letter that changed everything. It was from my biological father, who had been serving time in prison for crimes I still didn't fully understand. He got locked up when I was young. My memories of my father were a blurry mix. The letter was simple, written in his shaky handwriting. He apologized for the past, for the choices that had torn our family apart. He wanted to reconnect, to be a part of my life again. The words danced across the page, both hopeful and fragile.

I initially hesitated, staring at the letter for days. My mother rarely ever spoke of my biological father, which always made me wonder what other secrets she kept locked away. But something tugged at my heart. I had a longing for answers and closure. So, I wrote back, cautiously at first, then with increased emotion. Our correspondence began, a secret exchange of letters transcending his prison walls. He shared stories of his youth, of dreams deferred and roads taken that led to the shadows of missed birthdays and graduations. I absorbed every word, learning about the man behind the inmate number, his regrets, hopes, and raw vulnerability.

As I packed my bag for the weekend, I wondered how I'd kept my secret from everyone: my parents, girl, friends, and teammates. It was the irony of becoming a man while still feeling like a child. My friends assumed I was just another college basketball star navigating life's milestones. My mother believed I was focused on my studies and the court, oblivious to the letters that arrived in plain envelopes stacked on my desk. I wouldn't tell her. Not yet. She'd only see it as betrayal, a reopening of old wounds. In her eyes, I had the only father I'd ever need: Augustine Hill.

The sun's rays cast a golden hue over the car as I filled up my trunk with bottles of liquor. Next, I headed to campus to pick up Ava and hit the road. Midterms were finally over, and we both needed the break. I couldn't wait to turn up and unwind with my girl. The road to the beach house stretched ahead, winding through coastal towns and lush greenery. I stole glances at Ava every chance I could, her profile softened by the afternoon light. The anticipation of the weekend weighed on me, our private escape, the chance to unwind, and maybe, just maybe, to express what I felt. Being with her felt different. I couldn't help but feel myself falling for her, but I didn't want to scare her off.

I grinned. "You know, this drive reminds me of when I was a kid.

My dad used to take me to this very beach house. We'd roll down the windows, and the salty breeze would whip through the car. He'd play old R&B tunes, and we'd sing along like we were the only people in the world."

Ava leaned back in the passenger seat. "Sounds like a perfect memory."

"Yeah. Back then, blood couldn't make us any closer. He taught me how to fish off the pier, skip stones across the water, and appreciate the simple things."

Ava flashed me her bright smile. "That's dope. I'm glad you had that bond with him."

"And what about your family? You rarely talk about them."

She looked out the window. "Well, I'm the youngest of three girls. My parents are still together, which is rare these days. They've always been supportive, but my sisters—they're overachievers. One's a successful lawyer, the other a brilliant engineer. And then there's me, still figuring it all out. Sometimes I feel like the letdown of the family."

I reached across the center console and grabbed her hand. "Ava, don't say that. You're not a letdown, baby. You're unique, and your path doesn't have to mirror theirs. Besides, you've got time. Graduation isn't a deadline; it's a beginning. What do you want to do with your life?"

She squeezed my hand before responding. "I wish I knew. Maybe this weekend will help me find some clarity. Away from the noise, the expectations. Just us, the sun, and the waves."

"I'm sure it will."

As the miles rolled by, our conversation flowed. It was a blend of memories, dreams, and the promise of a quiet beach house waiting for us.

———

As we stepped through the weathered wooden door of the beach house, the air changed. It was a blend of saltwater, sun, and memories that clung to your skin and whispered secrets of summer's past. I dropped our bags near the entrance, and Ava kicked off her sandals. My nose caught a whiff of coconut-scented candles, which my mother always lit during our family vacations. It was a comforting aroma mixed with the smell of salt and sunscreen.

The beach house was a cozy yet modern refuge, its walls adorned with faded seashell prints and driftwood art. The sunlight streamed through the sheer curtains, casting dancing patterns on the wooden floor. The family room held a well-loved sofa, its cushions sunken from years of conversations, laughter, and afternoon naps. A bookshelf sagged under the weight of dog-eared novels and sand-filled photo albums. The kitchen boasted a view of the ocean. The window framed a postcard-worthy scene—the turquoise water meeting the sky. The bedrooms were simple: queen-sized beds with modern decor and paintings of seascapes and lighthouses.

We exchanged a knowing look and, without hesitation, headed straight for the sliding glass doors that opened onto the deck. The ocean beckoned, waves crashing against the shore like an old friend eager to catch up. The beach house stood perched on the edge of the dunes, its wooden deck overlooking the crashing waves. Ava wandered across the deck, her skinny brown fingertips grazing the wooden railing. The calm ocean stretched before her, a vast canvas of blues and greens. Seagulls swooped and called, and the horizon seemed infinite.

"This," she said softly. "Watching how the sun kisses the water is exactly what I needed. It's like time stands still here."

"Take all the time you need, baby. Stay right there. I got somethin' to make this even better."

I returned moments later with a pre-rolled blunt and lighter. Ava looked at me with a mischievous smile. The sun dipped low, creating a canvas of pink and orange hues across the waves as we sparked up the blunt I'd gotten from Jemal. I knew I shouldn't have been smoking, but I needed the release, and so did she. We passed the blunt back and forth, smoking it down to the end, and I realized that maybe love wasn't about saying it out loud. Maybe it was about sharing blunts over sunsets, the comfort in the quiet mornings, and a beach house that held more memories than my arms could contain.

The salty breeze swept through the open sliding doors, ushering in the scent of the ocean and marijuana. Inside, the air was thick with laughter and anticipation. We were both giddy, our senses heightened by the thrill of Mary Jane. My heart raced as I tiptoed across the living room, seeking the perfect hiding spot for our impromptu game of hide and seek. Ava covered her eyes and counted to twenty, her voice echoing through the house. I darted into the hallway, my bare feet padding silently on the hardwood floor. I squeezed into the linen closet, stifling a giggle. The door creaked shut, and I held my breath, listening for her footsteps.

"Ready or not, here I come!"

Her laughter floated down the hallway. She was close. My heart pounded as I peeked through the slats of the closet door. When she finally swung it open, I burst out, sprinting toward the kitchen. She chased after me, her laughter contagious as she remained hot on my trail. We circled the dining table, me ducking behind chairs while she lunged after me. Our playful wrestling sent us crashing into the wall. My shoulder slammed into the framed painting, which popped away from the wall, revealing a hidden safe behind the canvas.

Ava's eyes widened. "What's this?" she asked, her fingers brushing the edge of the safe door. "Lincoln, did you know this was here?"

I shook my head, still catching my breath. "No idea. It's probably just an old safe. Maybe the previous owners left something inside."

Ava's natural curiosity got the better of her. She tugged at the safe's handle, but it wouldn't budge. "We need a combination," she replied, scanning the room. "What could it be?"

"Yo, chill, Inspector Gadget. C'mon, let's go in the kitchen and take some shots," I suggested, hoping to get her mind off things. "It's my birthday, and I'm tryna turn up!"

"Whatever you say, birthday boy," she replied, following me into the kitchen.

Ava's brown eyes sparkled as she raised her shot glass, the amber liquid catching the warm glow of the overhead lights. "Happy birthday, Lincoln. Here's to finally being legal!"

I grinned, my cheeks flushed excitedly as I clinked my glass against hers. The shot burned down my throat, leaving a trail of warmth in its wake.

Ava reached across the island, her fingers brushing against mine. "You know, twenty-one is a magical age. It's like stepping into a whole new world. Have you thought about what adventures you want to have?”

I leaned back against the counter, thinking. “Hmm, I don’t know. Maybe I’ll take another spontaneous road trip witchu.”

“Booooo!” Ava laughed, her eyes crinkling at the corners. “You can think of something better than that.”

“I’m too high to think right now,” I confessed with a chuckle.

Before she could respond, the doorbell chimed. My heart raced. No one knew we were there.

“I’ll get it,” she offered before racing off to the door.

“Hold up,” I called out.

I stood a few paces behind her and watched her open the door. On the other side was an Instacart delivery person who handed her a cake box and a box of candles. The scent of chocolate wafted through the air, and my curiosity and excitement grew.

“What are you up to?” I queried.

“Follow me to the kitchen and see,” Ava teased, cutting me a mischievous glance from over her shoulder.

She placed the cake box on the kitchen island and popped open the box. My eyes widened as they fell upon the cake. Unbeknownst to me, Ava had planned a surprise celebration that would etch the day into my treasured memories forever. She’d selected a decadent chocolate cake adorned with swirls of buttercream frosting. The vibrant blue candles stood tall, waiting to be ignited. Ava lit them one by one, their flames dancing like miniature stars.

“Happy birthday,” she whispered, pulling me close. The taste of salt clung to my lips as we kissed, the cake waiting patiently in the background.

“You didn’t have to,” I told her, eyes shining joyfully.

“But I wanted to,” she replied. “Because you deserve all the sweetness in the world.”

“When did you even have time to do this?”

“Easy. I placed an Instacart order as soon as we got here.”

A smile spread across my face as I leaned in, whispering against her ear, “Best birthday ever. Thank you, baby.”

We sat side by side, slicing into the cake. Chocolate crumbs clung to our fingertips as our laughter spilled like champagne bubbles. The candles flickered, illuminating our brown faces before I made a wish and blew them out.

———

Later that night, the house was silent. Ava lay sprawled across the bed, her breathing steady. I couldn't sleep. The safe and the possibilities of what lay hidden behind its steel door haunted my thoughts. I tiptoed down the hallway, the moonlight casting shadows on the hardwood floor. My thoughts raced through the significant dates in my life as I tried to decipher the code to the safe. *Is it my birthday? My parents' wedding anniversary? My mother's birthday?* I spun the dial, trying each combination. The first two attempts yielded nothing. On the third try, the safe clicked open. My heart somersaulted in my chest as I swung the door wide.

Inside, nestled among velvet-lined compartments, were diamonds sparkling underneath my phone's flashlight. Stacks of crisp bills, all neatly bound with rubber bands, and plastic-wrapped bricks filled the remaining space. My breath caught in my throat. It was a fortune, a secret stash that could change my life forever. I eased the door shut, mind racing in a million different directions. The dollar signs danced before my eyes, and I *knew* I had to share the news with someone. I quickly dialed my boy Jemal's number. He answered on the third ring.

"What's good, my nigga? This better be a drunk dial, and yo' ass better be lit for your birthday!"

"Jemal," I whispered. "Listen to me. You won't believe what the fuck I just found."

Jemal listened intently as I spilled the story. The diamonds, the drugs, and the money were like something straight out of a movie. "Nigga!" Jemal exclaimed. "We've hit the mothafuckin jackpot."

I swept my hand over my coils. "How am I supposed to steal this shit? This is my family's beach house. Besides, I haven't even told Ava. She's sleep."

Jemal chuckled. "Lincoln, my friend, this is what we call hittin' a lick. What your girl don't know won't hurt her. We'll sell the diamonds, launder the cash, and flip those bricks to get more cash. No one will ever know. I mean, how many times do your people visit that beach house anyway? Ain't no tellin' how long that shit has been sitting there."

My conscience wrestled with greed. I glanced down the hall at the bedroom door where Ava slept peacefully. The safe's secrets weighed heavily on my shoulders. But the allure of wealth was intoxicating.

"If we do this, we do it when I say, and we do it right. I can't have it lookin' like I had a hand in this. It can't be traced back to me."

The Student

T *wo weeks later.*

The spring breeze tousled my hair as I hurried toward the library. My backpack weighed heavily on my shoulders, filled with textbooks and half-finished essays. And then, out of nowhere, there he was, Professor Hill, striding purposefully across the quad, coming straight toward me. His salt-and-pepper beard caught the sunlight, and his tailored suit accentuated his broad shoulders.

Eager to speak to him, I quickened my pace, heart fluttering. As badly as I wanted to deny my feelings, I was sick of admiring him from afar while secretly nursing a crush that defied reason. He was more than just handsome; he possessed an intellectual allure that reeled me in like a moth to a flame. All I wanted to do was break the invisible barrier that separated student from teacher.

"Professor Hill!" I called out, my voice echoing between the tall oak trees. He looked up, his eyes narrowing in recognition. I jogged over to him, my breath slightly uneven.

"Good morning, Miss Newman," he greeted me, his voice a rich baritone.

"Good morning."

"How was your time at the beach house during spring break? Did you find the clarity you were seeking?"

"Y-yes," I stammered, remembering all the weed Lincoln and I smoked and the hidden safe we'd found. "It was... enlightening."

His lips curved into a faint smile. "I'm glad to hear that."

"Have you gotten the chance to read my latest submission? I've been eager to hear your thoughts."

"No. Honestly, I've been passing off the last few assignments to Karina, my TA."

My heart sank. "Oh."

I could tell his mind was elsewhere. I sensed it in the curt tone of his response. I could feel the eyes of everyone we passed by on us.

"Well, I have to be going."

"Y-yeah, me too."

"Have a good day, Miss Newman."

"Yeah, thanks. You too, Professor Hill."

He breezed by me, and I turned and followed him toward the secluded corner of the courtyard, where the aging stone walls shielded us from prying eyes. I took a deep breath, my fingers brushing against his as I reached for him.

"Professor," I began, my voice barely audible. "You seem stressed. Is everything all right?"

He glanced at me, surprise flickering in his glare. "Stressed? Perhaps. There's always more to do than time allows."

I stepped closer, my body inches from his. "You don't have to carry it all alone," I murmured. "I'm here if you need... *help* relieving it."

His hardened gaze bore into mine, and for a moment, the world narrowed to just the two of us. "Ava," he said sternly. "Are you crazy? We've been through this—"

"I know, but I still think about you," I confessed, my cheeks aflame with shame as I looked down at the bulge behind his pleated slacks. "I know I shouldn't, but I do. I still want it, Professor."

His jaw tightened, and he looked away. "Ava, this isn't—"

"Professional," I finished for him. "I know. But sometimes, the heart doesn't listen to reason."

Instead of responding, he checked his watch, the seconds ticking away. "I have thirty minutes before my meeting with my TA. We can't—"

"We can," I insisted, my hand grazing his arm. "Just a quickie."

We threw caution to the wind and hurried into his office, the space where literature breathed, and forbidden desires would be fulfilled. The door clicked shut, sealing us in Professor Hill's dimly lit office. The air smelled of old books and anticipation. His eyes bore into mine, and I sensed a battle within him, the professional scholar and father versus his own carnal desires. I stepped closer, my fingers grazing his beard.

He shifted, his hand brushing mine. "Ava, I thought we agreed."

"This isn't about grades, Professor Hill. It's about longing, the ache that lingers between my thighs long after your class ends."

"I'm your professor, and Lincoln is my son," he murmured. "I shouldn't—"

"Feel this way?" I asked, my lips inches from his. "But you do. And so do I."

His resolve crumbled. He cupped my face, his touch electric. "Ava," he whispered, "I've dreamed of—"

"Fucking me all around this office," I finished my pulse throbbing.

His gaze was intense as he stared at me, the student who dared to challenge him, the woman who stirred emotions he tried so hard to bury. And then, our lips met, a violent collision of hunger and restraint. His kiss tasted of rage and vulnerability, and I quickly surrendered to the pull of our longing bodies. The dusty bookshelves witnessed our sin, the unraveling of boundaries, and the exploration of forbidden syllables.

My heart raced as he picked me up, set me on top of his cluttered desk, and started massaging my breasts before peeling off my shirt and bra. He brushed my hair behind my shoulder before kissing me. As the seconds passed, I felt myself falling violently from how he made my body tingle. A part of me wondered if what I felt for him was madness or fate, but I knew one thing: in those thirty minutes, I would unravel the layers of Professor Hill—the poet, the scholar, and perhaps, the man who longed for more than just academic conversation. I locked my legs around his waist while he hungrily sucked my nipples. I palmed the back of his head, feeling his wet tongue lapping at my flesh. He hurriedly pulled my panties to the side and licked my pussy as if he worshipped me.

"Yes, fuck! Oh, right there! Don't fuckin' stop, Professor! I'm gonna cum!" I squealed, eyelids flickering toward the ceiling in ecstasy.

I sat up on my elbows and watched him between my thighs, enjoying my front-row view as I bucked against his face. I screamed out in pleasure, soaking his salt-and-pepper beard with my sweet nectar. He swiftly unbuckled his pants, spread my legs from east to west, and pushed his rock-hard dick inside me without mercy. I held on for the ride, moaning and screaming with pleasure as he drilled into me.

"Holy fuck, Professor Hill! Your dick feels soooo gooood."

He held my legs in a locked position, each stroke deep and hard. My breasts jiggled as I watched him fuck me, the sweat beads on his brow, the merciless look on his face.

After he pounded my pussy, I dropped to my knees and took him into my mouth, looking up at him as I sucked. He had a scowl of pleasure on his face, eyes rolling back in his head as I deepthroated him. He palmed the back of my skull, ensuring the head of his dick tapped against the back of my throat.

"Mmm, shit, Little Dove," he growled.

He swiftly pulled me back to my feet and bent me over his mahogany desk. Like a dog to a fire hydrant, I propped one leg up, and he reentered me from behind. Professor Hill's strong hands gripped my waist, panting heavily. I reached around and spread my ass cheeks apart while bucking back against him. He forcefully gripped the back of my neck while the other hand gripped my indented waist.

He smacked my ass. "Oooh shit, you feel so fuckin' good!"

I swung my hair from one shoulder to another before looking back at him. "Mmm, shit. You feel too damn good, Professor. I'm gonna cum again!"

He leaned in closer, breath warm against my nape. "Mmm, shit. I like it when you talk that nasty shit." He kissed my neck and grabbed my breasts from behind. "Now take that fuckin' dick 'til you cum!" he demanded.

I stood on the tips of my toes, palms planted into the folders beneath me. "Mmm, yes! Fuck this pussy, Professor!"

Our short time together stretched by like taffy, each second a fragile thread that threatened to snap. Professor Hill nestled himself deep inside me, pumping relentlessly until we both climaxed. We clung to our stolen intimacy, lips reluctant to part. My heart raced as I gathered my clothes and quickly redressed. His office was hot like seven summers and somehow felt smaller, its walls closing in on our darkest secrets. A sharp knock echoed through the room as I reached for the doorknob. I froze. The timing was cruel—a cosmic joke played by fate. I glanced back at Professor Hill, who stood near the window, his expression unreadable.

"Come in," he called, his voice steady.

The door swung open, revealing Karina, his teaching assistant— bright-eyed, eager, and oblivious to the charged atmosphere. "Professor Hill," she stated, "I've compiled the midterm grades, and—"

"Thank you, Karina," he interrupted her. "Leave them on my desk."

Karina hesitated, her gaze flickering between the professor and me. "Is everything okay?"

"Everything is fine," he assured her. "Just a student consultation."

"I'll see you around, Professor Hill," I announced, slipping past Karina, leaving behind the subtle scent of sex.

I caught Karina's curious look, but the words remained lodged in her throat. The hallway swallowed me whole as I hurried down the corridor. My mind was a whirlwind of regret and longing as I tasted the bittersweet remnants of his kiss on my lips. I wondered if I'd crossed a line, but the thrill of forbidden proximity drowned my doubts. The campus buzzed with oblivious students as I headed toward the library with a smile. I carried a secret, a stolen sonnet imprinted into the depths of my soul.

THE TA

K arina Ahmed

The air smelled of sexual secrets that defied logic and academia. I could hear Ava's pulse racing as she slipped past me. I knew something was up. Professor Hill faced me, his eyes haunted.

"Karina," he said. "About those grades..."

"Yes, Professor Hill?" I asked, closing the door behind me. "Is there a problem?"

The professor's office was a cramped space, cluttered with stacks of papers, half-empty coffee cups, and the faint scent of old books. He took his seat behind his desk. "No. Not a problem. I just wanted to say thank you for really stepping up. I know I've been leaning on you a lot this semester, and for that, I apologize."

I dipped my chin. I was known for my efficiency and unwavering commitment to my duties. "It's no problem, sir. Was there anything else you needed?"

He swung his head in contempt. "No. Was there something you

wanted to discuss? I don't have my next student appointment for another forty-five minutes."

I hesitated, my mind spiraling. I had my own problems and burdens that weighed me down, like lead. I *needed* money. My father's illness had reached a critical stage. The cancer had ravaged his body, and the doctors offered little hope until now. He was eligible for a new experimental trial. It was risky, but it was also our *only* chance. The problem was we needed money fast. The trial had a narrow window, and if we missed it, he wouldn't qualify. The last thing I wanted to do was burden him with my personal woes, but I was desperate. Between the twenty-five thousand dollars we needed for the trial and the mountain of medical bills that drained our savings and threatened to bury my dreams of becoming a college graduate, I was drowning in debt.

I cleared my throat. "My father... You know we've been through a lot of ups and downs with his health. His doctors say he's eligible for a new experimental trial overseas. It may be our last hope to save him."

Professor Hill's expression softened. "Karina, I'm sorry to hear about your father. But why are you telling me this?"

I hesitated, then blurted out, "I need an advance on my salary. Just enough to cover the initial costs. I'll work extra hours, I promise."

He leaned forward, his brown gaze piercing. "And you think I can help?"

I drew in a deep breath. "I've heard rumors about an emergency fund, like a secret stash for dire situations. If you could—"

The professor interrupted, his voice low. "Karina, I can't promise anything, but I'll consider it. For you."

A ghost of a smile crept across my lips. "Thank you, Professor. I promise you won't regret it!"

I stepped out of the professor's office, the door closing behind me with a soft click. The hallway was empty as my footsteps echoed under my shadow. Each step felt like a ticking clock. My father's life hung in the balance, and I was racing against time. I clutched my phone, my mind a whirlwind of desperation and determination. Professor Hill's promise of considering an advance on my salary lingered like a fragile thread of hope.

Then my phone buzzed with a call from a familiar number. I hesitated, staring at the screen for a few seconds, then answered. "Hello?"

"Kit Kat, it's me," a familiar voice crackled through the line. It was Jemal, my younger brother, who'd always danced on the edge of trouble.

"What do you want, Jemal?" My voice was sharp. I loved him fiercely, but I couldn't afford any more distractions.

"I messed up, sis," Jemal confessed. "Robbed the wrong guys. They're after me."

My heart sank. "You idiot! You know we can't afford any more trouble!" I hissed.

"I did it for us, Karina," Jemal pleaded. "For Dad. You think I like this life? But we need the fast money."

I leaned against the cold wall, feeling lightheaded. "Where are you right now?"

"I'm safe. I need to lay low for a while."

"How long is a while, Jemal?"

"Until I can put my next plan in motion."

"*Plan*? What's your plan?"

"There's a job," Jemal replied cryptically. "A risky one. But it pays well. Enough to cover Dad's trial."

My stomach churned. I'd always been the responsible one who followed the rules. But desperation had a way of bending morality. "Tell me."

"I can't say over the phone," he insisted. "Meet me at our spot—the old science building near the library on campus—in an hour."

"Campus? You're here?" I inquired, looking over my shoulder.

"I told you I was safe."

I hesitated before finally agreeing. "Fine. But, Jemal, if this goes south—"

"I know," he interrupted. "We're in this together, right?"

"Right," I answered with a sigh before ending the call.

My heart thumped against my ribcage as I glanced back at the professor's office. Professor Hill's face flashed in my mind, his softened gaze, the promise of help. But Jemal was my family. And blood couldn't have made us any closer. In the Ahmed family, we put each other first. My trust in my kid brother was a precarious balance between loyalty and skepticism. As siblings, we shared a bond forged in hardship that ran deeper than blood ties. But Jemal's reckless choices had tested that trust repeatedly. I knew he hustled for our family, but I also recognized the danger behind his decisions.

I wanted to believe in Jemal's plan, to cling to the hope that he had a foolproof plan to save our father. The stakes were higher than ever. Our father's life, my scholarship, and our fragile future hung in the balance. Only time would reveal whether Jemal's desperate gamble would strengthen our bond or shatter it irreparably. I clung to my hope as my trust swayed between love and caution.

———

Walking toward our meeting spot, I wondered how far I'd go to save my father. How many lines I'd cross, how many secrets I'd bury. I was no longer just a teacher's assistant; I was a desperate sister, a fighter, and perhaps, a reluctant ally to my brother's dangerous scheme. My pulse quickened when Jemal arrived. His cold, dark eyes darted around, assessing our surroundings. His sienna-brown face was twisted with worry, but determination glimmered in his gaze. His brooding eyes, however scary, still held a charismatic intensity. They were deep pools of dark chocolate, revealing both mystery and weakness. Whenever he looked at me, it felt like he could see straight into my soul. I hated it, and at the same time, it was probably my favorite thing about him. His sienna brown complexion mirrored mine, rich and warm. On top of his head was a crown of cornrows with tightly coiled, springy ends with the sides and back shaved down into a fade. His minimal facial hair was meticulously groomed. A well-defined mustache graced his upper lip, adding a touch of maturity to his youthful features. Below, a goatee and sparse beard framed his mouth and jawline.

He was clad in a green and gold WBU hoodie, blending in with the sea of students proudly sporting our school's colors. At twenty, my baby brother stood at the cliff of adulthood with a dangerous blend of arrogance and juvenile curiosity.

"Are you sure no one followed you?" I asked.

"Chill. It's a campus full of kids here. Plus, look at what I got on. I blended right in."

"Fine. Now tell me, what's the plan?"

He glanced at me, then leaned in. "There's a job. I'm talking about diamonds, money, and drugs. We steal it, sell it, and split the money. We pay for Dad's trial and whatever part of your tuition not covered by your scholarship."

"And what about your scholarship?"

He sucked his teeth. "You know that shit is long gone. I don't need ball, and I don't need this school. This job right here is the jackpot, Kit Kat. I swear, our whole lives are gonna change after this one."

I side-eyed him with an immense amount of skepticism in my arched brow. "How'd you find out about this so-called 'jackpot' of a job?"

"Trust me, my intel is valid."

My thoughts were all jumbled up in the front of my brain at once. *A job?* It sounded dangerous, but desperation had my ass in a chokehold. "And if you get caught?"

Jemal's jaw tightened. "I won't. I've got an inside man. He'll help us. But we need to move fast."

"Who is your inside man?"

"The less you know, the better, Kit Kat."

"Don't Kit Kat me right now, Jemal. Be straight with me. Who is your inside man?"

He sucked his teeth before glancing over his shoulder. "It's Linc."

"Linc? As in Lincoln Adams?"

"Yeah."

"Whose house are you hitting with him, of all people?"

"It's his family's beach house. He was there for spring break and hit me up when he found all that shit. We've been cooking up this plan for the past few weeks. He wanna sit and wait for the right moment to strike and shit. I think his ass is just scared."

"Wouldn't you be? He's got a lot on the line, which is why I'm confused about why he brought this to you in the first place. How could he ever benefit from biting the hand that feeds him?"

"I wondered the same shit, but then I said fuck it. If I'm eating at the end of the day, I don't give a fuck who else is at the table with me if they not family."

Beneath all of his sickening bravado, Jemal knew the world wasn't fair. He'd seen too much to believe in honor or loyalty. The plan was nothing more than a means to an end—a way to flip fate like a coin. He'd take whatever was inside that safe, no questions asked.

I sighed as the wheels in my head started to churn. "We only have a month to get the money to enter Dad into the experimental trial. What makes you think he'll go through with it?"

"Trust me, he will."

"What makes you so sure, Jemal?" I quizzed, doubling down on my question.

"If you saw what I saw, you wouldn't be asking that. I see that nigga's pupils turn into dollar signs every time we rap about this shit."

"Did he say how much cash was in the safe?"

"It ain't just about the cash, Kit Kat. It's a literal fuckin' gold mine. I'm talkin' cash, diamonds, *and* drugs."

"Hold up. Drugs? What kind of drugs?"

"Pure white bricks," he confirmed.

My eyes popped wide. "Oh shit!"

Hearing about the drugs added another layer to an already twisted story. The drugs and stacks of cash were all the proof I needed to know that Professor Hill had some sort of illegal extracurricular activities of his own going down. Nobody's hands were clean. Not mine. Not my brother's. And definitely not Professor Hill's. My heart sprinted up to my throat as my thoughts spiraled deeper. *Can we pull this off?* Not only was Lincoln cool with Jemal, but Lincoln was also Cassandra's son. The last thing I wanted was for my despair to bleed into her life any more than it already had. Our bond was special. Cassandra and I were in a delicate situation, harboring feelings for each other when she was my doctor. I knew better than anyone that the boundaries between professional and personal relationships could be complex, but that didn't deter my feelings for her.

My realization of my feelings for Doctor Hill unfolded gradually. It started with subtle moments, a lingering gaze, a shared laugh, and a shared sense of comfort during my therapy sessions. Over time, I noticed my thoughts drifting toward her outside my appointments. My attraction to her wasn't out of my nature. I'd always preferred a woman's touch over a man's, but I hadn't openly dated a woman. Cassandra and I tried to avoid crossing into personal and romantic territory but couldn't. And with my father's health hanging in the balance, I had to weigh the risks. His frail face flashed before my eyes, the tubes, the helplessness. Before I knew it, I found myself nodding.

"Fine. But no violence. You get in, and you get out."

Jemal grinned. "Agreed. We're in this together, sis."

The word *together* sent a shiver down my spine. We'd navigated treacherous waters in the past in the name of love and were about to do it again for a chance to rewrite our family's fate. All I could do was pray our desperate alliance would save our father, even if it meant dancing on the edge of darkness.

THE WIFE

One week later.

I shut my umbrella as I stepped into the cozy Taste of Heaven Diner downtown on a chilly Monday evening. The familiar space smelled of freshly brewed coffee and the faint sizzle of bacon. The clatter of dishes and the low hum of conversations provided a comforting backdrop. I peeled off my coat and proceeded over to my favorite booth. It was the one by the window with a view of the rain-soaked streets. Across from me was Karina, the striking young woman with eyes that held secrets and a piece of my heart. She was a force of nature—confident, sharp-tongued, and fiercely protective of her family.

The rain tapped gently against the window, creating a soothing rhythm. The waitress came over with a piping hot pot of coffee in her hand, but I opted for tea instead. I stirred my tea absentmindedly, mixing in a packet of sugar as I kept my gaze fixed on Karina. We'd met there before, always after hours, when the world quieted down and the walls of professionalism blurred.

"Beautiful," I murmured, my voice low. "You're truly a beautiful young woman, Karina."

Her lips curved into a half-smile. "Flattery from my therapist? I'll take it."

She was being facetious. We both knew it was more than flattery. She was more than a patient. She was my guilty pleasure and mole wrapped up in one beautiful Eritrean bow. As my husband's teacher's assistant, she fed me morsels of information on my husband about his late nights at the university, like breadcrumbs leading to forbidden territory. It was a dangerous game, but I couldn't resist. Karina's allure was magnetic, her intelligence captivating. I often wondered if my husband ever noticed my absence during our secret rendezvous or if he was too caught up in his own world. As true as my connection to Karina was, I was fully aware of the boundaries. I loved my husband. He was the man who shared my bed and laughed at my silly jokes. No affair, no stolen kisses, or whispered promises could replace that. No matter how good her pussy was, I'd never leave him or the life we'd created together.

"You'd look good with my son," I said, my tone playful yet pointed.

Karina raised an arched brow. The unspoken tension hung heavy in the air. "You know I only have eyes for you, Cassandra."

"You know I'm married," I replied, glancing down at my wedding ring.

Karina's manicured fingers traced the rim of her coffee cup. "And you know I'm in love with you."

A sigh escaped my lips. Perhaps it was during one of our many vulnerable conversations or a moment of emotional connection that she recognized her feelings for me. They were a cocktail of genuine attraction, the need for emotional support, and the projection of unmet maternal needs. I hadn't been able to place a timestamp on when my own feelings blossomed. I'd been trained to maintain professional boundaries with patients for ethical and effective treatment. My role had gone from primarily therapeutic with her to so much more. We were both in too deep without a clear way out.

I sipped my tea before finally responding. "Believe it or not, but your well-being is my *only* priority. And if your feelings for me are becoming too overwhelming, I can refer you to a different therapist."

Her brows snapped together. "A different therapist? Are you serious right now, Cassandra? C'mon, we both know I make you feel better than he ever could."

As true as her words may have been, my mind had already been made. Karina's sepia-brown eyes quickly became red-rimmed, her hands trembling as she clutched her mug. I'd seen many distressed patients over the years, but something about her vulnerability, in particular, tugged at my heartstrings. I leaned forward, my voice gentle yet persistent.

"Karina, I've been carefully considering our sessions together. You've shared so much with me, and I appreciate your trust. But I think it's time for me to refer you to one of my colleagues who can provide more targeted care for your specific needs. Maybe you'd even like to consider group therapy sessions."

Her gaze dropped to her lap as her fingers traced the rim of her coffee cup. "But *you've* been helping me," she whispered. "I thought... I thought *we* were making progress."

I sighed inwardly. As a professional and a woman, I knew my limitations. "I mean it when I say I care about your well-being. And sometimes, the best care means seeking expertise beyond my own. You deserve that, Karina. I want that for you."

Her tears spilled over, and I hesitated. Instinctively, I reached out, my hand hovering above hers. But then I pulled back. *Boundaries are crucial, Cassandra, especially in moments like these,* I reminded myself. *If you care about her, you'll pull back.*

Karina slipped out of the booth and abruptly got to her feet. "I can't do this anymore," she choked out. "I thought you understood."

Rain pelted against the diner's window, blurring the world outside. The diner's bell chimed as Karina swung the door open and disappeared into the gray downpour. My heart clenched. *You can't let her leave like this.* I quickly dug inside my purse and tossed a few crumpled bills onto the table to cover our drinks, not bothering to count them. Grabbing my coat and umbrella, I dashed after Karina, my designer heels slipping on the wet pavement.

"Karina, wait!" I called, catching up to her just outside the diner.

She turned to me, her sweet face streaked with rain and tears. "What do you want?"

My breath came in ragged gasps. "I want to help you," I answered, my voice raw.

She scoffed. "Like you give a fuck. Stop messing with my emotions because you're unsure of your own!"

My chest deflated with a long sigh. "At least let me drive you back to campus. You shouldn't be standing out here in the rain."

Karina hesitated, her gaze searching my face. Then, without a word, she nodded. I popped open my umbrella, and we huddled underneath it. I tossed my arm around her, pulling her close as the raindrops tapped in a steady rhythm overhead. As we climbed into my car, I knew I was crossing a line. But sometimes, empathy demanded more than my professional detachment. As I drove through the rain-soaked streets, I stole glances at Karina. She sat huddled in the passenger seat, her tear-streaked face illuminated by the dashboard lights. The silence between us offered solace where our words fell short.

The rain drummed relentlessly against my car roof, a ceaseless rhythm that matched my turmoil. The diner had become a distant memory, replaced by the urgency of the moment. The red light seemed to stretch into eternity. My knuckles whitened as I gripped the steering wheel. I had always been a by-the-book professional before Karina fell into my life. She was the first patient to demand that I break the rules, and I willingly complied. Her pain was visible and understandable. The weight of her sadness pressed against my chest.

When the light finally turned green, I hesitated. The campus was only a few miles away. It was a safe and familiar destination for both of us. But something in Karina's eyes made me reconsider. I couldn't send her back to the dorm, back to the loneliness and despair that awaited her there, knowing I'd broken her heart. Instead, I made a split-second decision. I veered left, away from the direction of campus, and drove back toward the heart of the city. Rain blurred the windshield, and the wipers worked overtime. Karina didn't ask questions; she simply stared out at the wet streets, lost in her own thoughts.

Ten minutes later, I pulled into the parking lot of a modest hotel.

The neon sign flickered, casting an otherworldly glow. "Get out, Karina. We're staying here tonight," I announced, voice steady.

Karina shifted to face me, confusion etching lines on her face. "But—"

"No buts," I interrupted. "You need a break. A respite from everything. Just one night." I reached for my purse, fumbling for my wallet. "I'll cover the cost. Consider it... therapeutic."

"Why are you doing this?"

I met her gaze. "Because sometimes, healing isn't just about therapy sessions and referrals. It's about human connection. Tonight, we're just two people seeking shelter from the storm."

We stepped out into the rain, sharing the umbrella once more. The hotel lobby smelled of old carpet and disinfectant. The receptionist raised an eyebrow at our dampened appearance, but I didn't care. I handed over my credit card, signing the receipt with a swish of my wrist. As we rode the creaky elevator to the third floor, Karina's shaky hand brushed against mine. The touch was brief, but it spoke volumes. I turned up the heat inside the room, draped towels over the chairs, and placed a room service order for two cups of chamomile tea. When it arrived, we sat on the edge of the bed, sipping the sweet warmth in silence.

"You're not like other therapists," Karina whispered.

I smiled. "Maybe not. But tonight, I'm just Cassandra. And you're Karina. No titles, no expectations."

The rain continued to fall outside, a lullaby for our wounded souls as she stepped closer to me, blurring the lines a little more. Karina's nimble fingers trembled as she unbuttoned my rain-slicked coat. It fell to the floor, revealing the vulnerability beneath. My pulse galloped.

"Tell me, Cassandra," Karina whispered, her soft lips brushing against my earlobe. "What do you want?"

I hesitated, torn between duty and desire. I was a psychologist. I'd been trained to dissect emotions, yet I was entangled in an emotional web of my own creation. With each passing second, I felt my morality dissolving like sugar in hot tea. I'd never been one for impulsive decisions, but Karina always seemed to be the exception to the rule. I knew we were playing with fire, but the flames were intoxicating. At times, I craved Karina's touch more than my next breath.

"I want you," I admitted. "All of you... but this... it has to be the last time."

Karina's eyes darkened as she stepped closer. Her hands traced the curve of my waist, leaving a trail of fire. "What about Professor Hill? I told you what I think he's been up to. Doesn't that mean anything to you?"

"It means everything to me, but can we please not talk about him? Karina, my husband's not here right now, and he's not you."

Karina's laughter was bitter. "Say I'm better than him."

"Karina, I—"

"Say it," she demanded, grabbing my chin and pulling my face close to hers.

"Not better, Karina. *Different.* You're fire and chaos. Your pussy is the forbidden fruit I can't fuckin' resist."

Our lips met, a soft collision of longing and guilt. I tasted the coffee she had at the diner, the rain on her brown skin. Our bodies melted together, seeking solace in each other's familiar warmth as I laid her against the plush hotel room bed. Our tongues danced a familiar waltz around each other's mouths. I straddled her as her eager fingertips skated underneath my shirt and up the small of my back. She unhooked my bra before lifting my shirt over my head and gently sliding the straps from my shoulders. Next came her clothes. I lifted her shirt to reveal her black lace bra and stripped her of them. As her clothes fell, one article after another, so did our inhibitions. I licked my lips, silently admiring her bare upper body before my lips latched around her hard nipple like a moth to a flickering flame. My hand lingered against the top of her round ass while her sweet moans filled the air.

"Let me taste you," she whispered through panting breaths.

She rolled me over onto my back, taking control. Karina suckled my nipples while massaging my throbbing pussy through my panties.

I tossed my head back with a smile. "Mmm, shit."

I sat up on my elbows, watching her kiss my inner thigh. She pulled my panties to the side and kissed my clit. The sound of her tongue slurping against my flesh was enough to push me straight over the edge.

I sucked in air through my teeth as a moan escaped my lips. "Oooh my God."

She rolled me over onto my stomach, and I popped my ass in the air so that she could slide my panties down. Karina wasted no time diving in to eat my pussy and ass from behind as if she were on death row and I was her last meal.

I bounced my ass against her face, smearing my makeup against the crisp, white sheets. "Oooh shit. Oh my God, yes! Karina, yes! Lick that cat, baby," I purred, reaching back to spread my ass cheeks open. "Fuck! You feel so good I'm gonna cum!"

She continued to suck and slurp my clit like a 7-Eleven Slurpee as I jiggled my ass against her lips. As soon as I came, we switched positions. My hands mapped Karina's perfectly sculpted curves, the sharp angles of her collarbones, and the softness of her butterscotch thighs. The scars on her wrists told stories of silent battles fought and dark secrets kept. I kissed each one, eager to consume every bit of her. Karina palmed the back of my head as I slurped her hairless honeypot.

I explored her body with my tongue, whispering my deepest secrets against her folds. Her body was a canvas, a beautiful map of desire and delight. Her sparkling brown eyes held galaxies as she stared at me from between her thighs.

"I love you, Cassandra. I love you so much," Karina declared through her moans.

"Shh. All I wanna do is make you feel good," I whispered while licking her soft folds.

In my mind, it was our final fuck. I had no choice but to make it count. She moaned as I tongue fucked her clit, kissing it as she bucked against my face.

Karina whimpered in pleasure while squeezing her thighs around my head. "Oooh shit! Yes! Yes! You feel so good I'm gonna cry."

"You taste so fuckin' good."

I pushed her legs up in the air to devour her pussy more. She gripped a handful of my hair as I slid my tongue up and down her slit just how she liked it until her body shook with pleasure.

I reached up to grab her breasts. "Mmm, it's so fuckin' wet."

Soon, the air smelled of lavender and secrets. I lost myself in

Karina, falling deeper for how her breath hitched and her nails sifted through my roots. We entwined our limbs, winding our hips against each other in a desperate and hungry motion. I saw stars when I climaxed, unraveling years of restraint. Our bodies collapsed against the bed, chests heaving in and out. Our lovemaking had been a fragile flame burning against the darkness I didn't want to end. When I got to the other side of that door, I'd have to put my professional mask back on for good.

———

Karina hurried to the shower to get cleaned up when my phone vibrated. My eyes darted to the screen. A photo of Augustine and I on our last trip to Dubai stared back at me.

"Shit," I hissed, instantly remembering our plans.

I'd forgotten them in the haze of lust. Yet, my real life demanded attention. I quickly got dressed while tossing the phone on the bed and letting it ring until my voicemail picked up. I slid my coat over my shoulders before stepping into the steamy bathroom.

"I have to go," I announced. "It's him."

I watched her running her bare hands over her naked, wet body. If I stared too long, I knew I'd never leave. Karina held the showerhead in her hand, rinsing away the soap from her body before she pushed open the frosted glass shower door and stared at me. Her eyes were unreadable, but she knew the rules. She was the TA, the secret keeper, the woman who fed me forbidden knowledge. But she also stripped me of my professional armor and made me bare my soul.

She finally nodded. "I understand."

"Remember, the room is paid for. It can still be your personal sanctuary for the night. Stay and rest," I insisted before my lips brushed against her damp forehead.

Her smile was bittersweet. "Goodnight, Doctor Hill."

I dipped my chin. "Goodnight."

I stepped into the hallway, my pulse racing as I hurried to the parking lot. Outside, the rain still fell as I slipped into my car. The raindrops tapped against my windshield as I started the engine and returned

Augustine's call. After the third ring, his voice crackled through the Bluetooth speaker, asking about our dinner plans.

"Are we still on tonight, baby? I'm at the event, and you're nowhere to be found."

I smiled, my heart divided, split between my loyalty to the man I loved and my desire for a woman who whispered odes of love between my thighs.

"I'll be there soon, baby," I assured him. "Just a little delayed."

———

I adjusted my rearview mirror as I navigated the rain-slicked road toward the campus visitor center. The Mid-Year WBU Faculty Mixer allowed colleagues to reconnect and share research updates and gossip once they were liquored up. We had to show our faces to ensure we weren't the center of the chatter train. As Augustine and I settled into our academic roles, the mixers became our little escapes from grading papers and committee meetings. Before joining the gathering, I decided to stop by my office. I needed a moment to freshen up. I still tasted Karina on my tongue and could smell her scent on my skin, which was branded on me like a fresh tattoo. My office was a cozy nook on the third floor of the health building. On the door was a small brass plaque with my name: Dr. Cassandra Hill.

Inside, the light illuminated stacks of research journals and a framed photo of Augustine and me on our wedding day. I kicked off my sensible flats and padded to the tiny bathroom in the corner. I splashed cool water on my face, the droplets refreshing my skin. I studied my reflection—my freshly cut and straightened bob framing my face, roots lifted and wavy from being sweated out. I reached into my bag and pulled out a comb, neatly smoothing my unruly strands. As I worked the brush through my hair with one hand, I pulled out my perfume and spritzed my body from head to toe, masking the smell of Karina with the scent of blooming magnolias.

I parked my car near the visitor's center, where the mingling inside had already begun. The building stood tall, its rain-speckled glass walls reflecting the surrounding trees. I saw my colleagues clustered in small groups, sipping wine and likely discussing everything from Shakespearean sonnets to which department had the most professors in rehab, or as the WBU president called it, "sabbatical." Inside, I spotted Augustine near the refreshment table, his crimson red tie slightly uneven. His eyes lit up when he saw me, and I crossed the room to join him.

"Cass," he said, pulling me into a warm hug. "You look stunning."

I blushed, feeling a mix of pride and affection. "Despite the rain."

"Mother Nature's got nothin' on you, bae."

"And you, my dear poet, look handsome yourself."

He grinned. "Thank you."

"So, catch me up. What did I miss?" I quizzed, grabbing a glass of champagne from one of the trays from a waiter passing by.

"Nothing so far, just your basic bullshit small talk. Tell me we don't have to spend our entire night here this time."

"We don't. I'm kind of tired anyway."

"Why were you late anyway?"

"Oh, um, I got caught up with a patient," I answered before sipping from my glass.

"Anything serious?"

I shook my head. "No. Everything's under control."

As the evening unfolded, we listened to our colleagues' animated conspiracies about the funding issues and shared snippets of their latest research projects. Later, under the starlit sky, we stepped outside, our hands naturally finding each other. I leaned against him, tipsy from too much champagne. Feeling the warmth of his presence made me smile. The misty night air was cool as Augustine helped me into the passenger seat of his car. The mixer had been a surprisingly delightful blur of laughter, academic gossip, and—perhaps a tad too much champagne. My cheeks were flushed, and my laughter spilled like the bubbles in my champagne glass.

"Home?" he questioned, his eyes crinkling at the corners.

His hand brushed against mine as he started the engine. Soon after, the campus receded in the side mirror. I glanced back at my abandoned vehicle on campus. *We'll get my car tomorrow.* I rested my head against the headrest.

"Home sounds good. But you know what sounds better?"

Augustine arched an eyebrow. "What's that?"

I giggled, my inhibitions floating away with each passing mile. "Flirting. Shameless, tipsy flirting."

His grip on the steering wheel tightened. "Oh? And what kind of flirting are we talking about?"

"Dirty, nasty flirting," I whispered, my voice sultry.

He glanced at me, his eyes sparkling with desire. "You're adorable when you're tipsy."

"Adorable?" I pouted. "Damn. I was going for irresistible."

He reached over, brushing a strand of hair behind my ear. "Mission accomplished, Mrs. Hill."

My laughter bubbled forth in the dim glow of the car's interior. The champagne had loosened my tongue a little too much. "Baby, did you see Professor Rodriguez tonight? That red dress—"

He chuckled, glancing at me. "I noticed."

My fingers traced the edge of the cold window. "I mean, seriously. How can someone look that good in a dress? It's like she stepped straight off somebody's runway."

"Are you jealous, Mrs. Hill?"

I faked my offense. "Jealous? *Me*? No, no. Just... admiring her physique."

He grinned. "Or maybe you're secretly attracted to her."

I leaned closer to him as the car slowed at the red light. "Maybe I am. Or maybe I'm just plotting to steal her personal trainer," I whispered playfully, breath warm against his cheek.

The car slowed as we approached the house. My heart skittered, not just from the champagne but from the thrill of our playful dance. I unbuckled my seat belt, leaning closer to my husband. I hadn't felt the gravitational attraction that strong between us in a long time. He parked the car, turning to face me. Without speaking, my lips met his, the taste of champagne lingering on my lips.

My liquid courage encouraged me. "I want you tonight," I announced after breaking the kiss.

Augustine grinned. "I'm all yours."

THE STUDENT

I strolled across the bustling campus toward Professor Hill's evening lecture. The fading sun was a few warm hues away from disappearing. The aroma of sizzling tacos and garlic fries wafted past my nose from the row of food trucks parked near the lecture hall. Students queued up, waiting in line for comfort food. I considered grabbing a snack but opted to finish the iced coffee cradled in my hand instead. I sipped my drink, letting the cold liquid energize me, when my phone vibrated in my pocket. I looked to see my older sister Vanessa's name flash on the screen.

I took a deep breath before answering. "Hey, Nessa. What's up?"

"Baby Newman! I've been waiting for you to call me back for days. How's the final semester treating you?"

I halted and rolled my eyes at the nickname she'd been calling me since I was a kid. I was the youngest in my family, the baby. Vanessa was the golden child, and our sister Jasmine was the tomboy. "It's... intense, but I'm surviving. But since you asked, I want to talk about something. Graduation is around the corner, and I'm lost."

"Lost?" she probed firmly. "Ava, you're getting a degree in communications. You're talented. You can't afford to be lost. What's your game plan come May?"

A long sigh eased out. "Well, I thought about freelancing, maybe ghostwriting children's books. Or traveling and finding some inspiration abroad. But—"

She cut me off. "But nothing, Baby Newman. This isn't a fairy tale. You need stability. Bills won't pay themselves. You can't freelance your way through life."

I could feel the weight of her words pressing down on me. She wasn't wrong, but dammit if I didn't want her to be. "I know, but—"

"No *buts*. I know I still call you the baby, but you're not a kid anymore. You're an adult. You need a job, a career. What's your backup plan if freelancing doesn't pan out?"

Backup plan? Fuck. I'd barely thought of a solid first plan for after graduation. I sucked my teeth. "It's not like I haven't been applying for jobs, Nessa."

"Any bites?"

I sighed before restarting my walk to class. "Not yet. I have a couple of virtual interviews scheduled, though."

"Good, because I'm telling you, don't put all your eggs in that freelancing basket. Being a starving artist may sound cute, but it's not. I worked my ass off to become a veterinarian. Sacrificed nights, weekends. You think I enjoyed it? Hell no. But now I have stability, a future."

"Stability isn't everything, Ness. I don't want to be trapped in a cubicle, suffocating. I want to—"

She sighed into the receiver, sympathizing. "Ava, I get it. But life is going to knock you on your ass if you're not prepared—job security, health insurance, retirement plans. It's on you if you take the free game or not."

"I'm scared, Nessa. I mean, what if I choose wrong? What if—"

"Ava, it's okay to have dreams, but you need to have a safety net, too. Have a full-time gig and freelance on the side. Travel but also save for emergencies. It's all about balance, bitch."

I chuckled. "Balance, got it."

Vanessa was a true mother hen. She'd always been driven, practical, and hell-bent on guiding Jasmine and me toward stable paths.

"Seriously though, you're smart and talented, and you've got Jas and me. Together, the three of us will help you figure it out."

I took a final sip of my iced latte just before approaching the lecture hall. "Thanks, Nessa. But I gotta go. I've got class," I informed her as I adjusted my book bag and headed toward the illuminated doorway.

"Anytime, Baby Newman," she replied before ending the call.

———

After class, Professor Hill's classroom emptied as I closed my laptop and shoved it inside my book bag. I shifted to see Karina standing there, her footsteps silent like a ninja.

She leaned against the desk next to me. "It's Ava, right?"

"Uh, yes."

"Mmm. You're not as low-key as you think."

"Excuse me?" I asked, brows snapping together as I swung my book bag over my shoulder.

"Your lingering glances during Professor Hill's lectures. They're not lost on me."

My breath hitched. "I—I don't know what you're talking about."

"Oh, but you do. The way you lean forward, hanging on his every word. The subtle brush of your fingers when he returns your assignments. It's all there."

I gave her a onceover. Karina's demeanor was as cold as a frost-kissed windowpane. Her eyes held secrets, and her words cut like shards of broken glass.

"It's admiration!" I replied defensively. "His lectures weave magic! It's simply respect for his brilliance."

Karina scoffed. "Admiration, huh? Let's call it what it is—an inappropriate crush. You think you're discreet, but I caught on. And trust me, others will, too. Unless you're cool with everybody knowing you're fucking your way to an A."

"Who the fuck do you think you are?"

She chuckled. "I've seen your grades change. And trust me, your writing hasn't improved *that* much."

"I've worked hard!"

"Bullshit! You go from penning paper porn to suddenly, your prose blossoms like spring flowers. That's not fucking talent. It's desperation."

I narrowed my gaze at her. "Why the hell do you even care?"

"Because I won't let you tarnish his reputation. You're not the first student to fall for those poetic brown eyes. But you'll be the last if I have anything to say about it."

"Is that a threat?"

She rolled her neck. "He's married, you know? Or does he take his ring off before you bust it open for him in his office?"

I kissed my teeth. Her imaginary beef with my ass had thrown me for a serious loop. "What's your problem? Why are you—"

She cut me off. "But I guess nobody fucks you better than a nigga you ain't supposed to be fuckin', right, *Little Dove*?"

Karina turned on her heels before I could respond, leaving me caught in a hurricane of emotions.

———

I stood there, my feet cemented to the ground, my heart pounding like a trapped bird. The professor's office door loomed ahead. I was too livid not to confront him and unravel the tangled threads of accusations from his assistant. With trembling fingers, I knocked. The door creaked open, revealing Professor Hill, his brown eyes weary from grading papers. His gaze lingered on mine, and I momentarily forgot about Karina's harsh words.

"Professor Hill, may I come in?"

He gestured me in with a quick wave. "What's on your mind, Little Dove?"

I shuddered at the nickname he'd given me as I stepped inside. The weight of unspoken words hung in the air. I glanced at the framed photograph on his desk, his smiling wife, and his hand intertwined with hers. I hadn't noticed it the last time I was in there. I was probably too caught up in lust.

"It's Karina, your TA. She just accused me of... seeking an easy way to an A. She basically said my work was trash!"

He leaned back in his chair. "Karina has a sharp tongue. But you're a talented writer, Ava. Your poems resonate."

"Is that all they do? Resonate?"

He studied me before responding. "Listen to me. Karina sees what she wants to see. She's seen other students fall, but you're different."

"Different how?"

"Because when you write, I can see what lies beneath. I know your syllables ache for more than petty metaphors."

"Then tell her she's wrong! Go to bat for me!"

"Poetry thrives on complication, Ava."

I rolled my eyes. "So basically, you're no help."

"I didn't say I wouldn't help—"

I stormed out of his office, wondering if Karina was right. Did the other students see me as the girl who laid on her back to pass Professor Hill's class? Her accusations danced in my head like dark sugarplum fairies as thoughts of the professor's wife waiting for him beyond the walls engulfed me in shame.

———

Later that night, I sat on my bed, hair disheveled and feeling emotionally drained. I looked around at the notebooks scattered around me as I wiped my tear-stained cheeks. My phone vibrated with an unsaved number dancing across the screen. I hesitated before letting it go to voicemail. Seconds later, it vibrated again.

"H-hello?" I answered, voice trembling.

"Little Dove," Professor Hill replied.

I wiped my tears before pulling the phone away from my ear to look at the number again. "H-how did you get my number?"

"I pulled it from your student file. I apologize if that feels intrusive."

"It does."

"Listen, I'm calling because I want to apologize. I'm parked outside your dorm. Can you come outside?"

My heart raced as I darted off the bed and over to my window, peering twelve floors to the ground. "Why? What's the point?"

"A real man always apologizes face-to-face. I promise I just want your conversation tonight. That's all."

I grabbed my jacket and keys and stepped into the chilly hallway.

Outside, Professor Hill's BMW waited, engine purring. I climbed into the car.

He glanced at me before pulling away from the curb. "I apologize for the intrusion, Little Dove. Thank you for coming."

We glided through the darkened streets as I sat cradled in his leather seat, feeling a mashup of excitement and conflict. I glanced at him, secretly fangirling over how he gripped the steering wheel.

"Professor Hill, why are we doing this? Why did you pull me out of my dorm late at night? And where are we going?" I probed as we weaved along the winding moonlit roads.

"I told you I wanted to apologize."

"Then why haven't you?"

"Do you trust me?"

"I don't trust anyone, Professor Hill."

"Touché." Soon after, his BMW halted at what felt like the edge of the world. "We're here."

I stepped out, my breath stolen by the view. The beautiful waterfall cascaded down, silver threads against the black canvas of the night. "Why here?" I inquired, shivering.

"Because waterfalls hold secrets. They swallow our confessions and echo them back as whispers," he replied, taking his place beside me.

I twisted my neck in his direction, noticing the moonlight-etched lines on his face. "So, about that apology, Professor Hill."

He chuckled. "Yes. I apologize for Karina's words. She's a storm, but like all storms, she'll pass."

I folded my arms across my chest. "You didn't see her, Professor. She said—"

"That you sought an easy A. That you were my muse. Don't let her get under your skin. I'll handle it."

"So you were actually listening when I came to you earlier."

"Of course, Little Dove."

"Can I ask you something?" I inquired.

"What's on your mind?"

I tilted my head. "*Little dove*? Why do you call me that?"

"Because you're my little dove, the one who flies higher than she realizes. But you're also fragile, like porcelain," he answered before I felt the sweet brush of his lips against my forehead.

"I never knew you thought of me that way."

He stepped closer, and the waterfall roared, drowning our voices. He pressed his lips against mine, the taste of our secret language lingering on his lips. I knew no matter what happened, we'd always find solace in each other's arms.

Professor Hill laced his fingers with mine as we approached the edge. "But we can't continue. Not like this."

I sighed, tearing my eyes to the ground. He'd been right about me being fragile. My heart had been severed into shards of longing for someone I could never truly have. "I know."

"You have Lincoln and a chance at something real."

I huffed. "And you're married."

"We can't keep betraying them. This is our last night together, Ava. Our final verse."

"We've said this before, y'know? What if this is the universe's way of telling us it doesn't want us to end?"

"This isn't up to the universe."

"Well, if this is the end, let me feel you one last time," I whispered against his ear.

Professor Hill kissed me, and the waterfall roared louder, swallowing our moans. We unraveled beneath the moonlight, just two souls caught between love and loyalty.

THE PROFESSOR

The phone on my mahogany desk buzzed, interrupting the silence of my study. I tapped accept, eyes narrowing as I listened to the police chief's gravelly voice on the other line.

"Augustine," Potomac Falls Police Chief Desmond Wilkinson began, "I wouldn't usually call you, but we've got your guy in for a bar fight. The guy he injured is in the hospital singing like a fuckin' canary."

I leaned back in my leather chair, fingers tapping rhythmically on the polished wood. "I appreciate the heads-up, Desmond," I replied, voice icy. "Hold him in a private cell with no cameras. I'll be there shortly."

Twenty minutes later, I stepped inside the police station, a menace lurking beneath the tailored suits and silk ties. It smelled of cheap coffee and poor choices. I strode down the narrow corridor with an armed officer beside me, our footsteps echoing off the cinderblock walls. The fluorescent lights flickered, casting shadows against the linoleum floor.

"Give us a minute," I told the officer as we approached a dimly lit cell.

Inside sat Vinny, his eye swollen. He'd always been a hothead. He got the scar that ran from his left eye to his chin after being sliced across the face with a bottle during an altercation when we were teenagers.

He'd been loyal to me for years, but this time, he'd crossed a line. The bar fight had drawn too much attention, especially for someone at his level in the game. I was too close to retiring and handing him the keys to the entire empire for his impulsive actions to have me second-guessing myself.

He looked up as I approached, rebelliousness in his eyes. "Don't even fuckin' say it, Brains."

I leaned forward, fingers gripping the rusted metal bars. "Vinny... What. The. Fuck?" I challenged, my voice a low growl.

"I said I don't wanna hear that shit."

My head wagged in disappointment. "You've always been loyal, but your loyalty means nothing if it blinds you to the bigger fuckin' picture. Unnecessary heat ain't gonna be good for nobody. C'mon, Vinny. Think!"

He scoffed. "I ain't forgot the bigger fuckin' picture, Brains. I'm the one who helped you create it."

"Then act like it, Vincent. Because I can't fuckin' tell from this side of the bars."

"Brains, you don't understand. I had to—" He explained, his voice raspy.

I raised a hand, silencing him. "You *had* to? Did that mothafucka you put in the hospital put a gun to your head and make you beat his ass? You think this is still the year 2000, and we're still throwin' bows in some back alley? We're an empire now, Vinny! I know you think you're invincible, but you're not. And your petty vendettas are gonna tear down this entire operation!" I hissed.

Vincent's jaw clenched. "Turn your bass down, mothafucka!" he barked back. "It was personal. He disrespected—"

"Disrespected?" I cut him off, narrowing my eyes. "You think this is about respect? This is about power. The power we've spent decades building. And you jeopardized it all over what?"

His gaze dropped to the concrete floor. "I had to show them."

My voice rose, echoing. "Show them what? Weakness? Because that's exactly what you showed me. Vinny, you know your role. You're at the top of the food chain. You keep our enemies in check and ensure our deals go smoothly."

Vinny grunted, shifting on the hard cot. "Yeah, well, you get shit done how you get it done, and I handle my grievances by getting my hands dirty, so you don't have to, *Professor*."

I narrowed my eyes. "All I care about is not disrupting the balance and the delicate fuckin' dance we perform to keep this fuckin' city under our thumb. Imagine if I hadn't gotten the call from Wilkinson."

His swollen fists clenched and unclenched. "Yeah, well. I guess we're both glad you did."

I signaled for the guard as I turned to leave. Vinny's voice followed me. "Brains," he called out. "What about the mothafucka in the hospital runnin' his mouth?"

I glanced back. "I'll handle it. Witnesses are a bitch."

———

My study was tucked away in the back of the house on the main floor. It was my sanctuary, where alliances and deals were inked in blood. I sat behind my massive mahogany desk that dominated the center of the room, its wood darkened by years of cigar burns. A humidor carved from ebony sat on the right. It held cigars rolled by Cuban hands, each one authentic. I lit one during critical moments, enjoying how the smoke curled in the air like clenched fists. A crystal liquor cart stood against the far wall, stocked with aged cognac and bourbon.

A few days passed since Vincent's arrest. I let him spend one night in that cell then put money on his bail and picked him up the next morning. He was right about one thing. He had his way of handling things, and I had mine. And at my age, I didn't enjoy getting my hands dirty like I used to. Instead, I called in a few favors at the hospital where the man Vincent assaulted was, found out his address, and hired somebody to run down on him the night he got released and put two bullets in the back of his skull. What was bad for Vincent was bad for me, too.

I opened my humidor to retrieve a cigar, cut it, and lit it. After exhaling two perfect smoke rings into the air, my phone rang.

"You called earlier?"

"Yeah. I did."

"What's the situation?" Vincent probed, speaking in a hushed tone.

I pressed the phone to my ear as I paced the hardwood floor inside my study. "Vinny, it's Brains. I want to discuss the upcoming shipment with you. This is a private line, so we can speak freely."

"Okay. What's up?"

"You remember the last time, all the last-minute chaos. I had to have Lincoln step in, but he got the wrong idea. He thought I was grooming him for the family business. You know how eager he can be, but a bit impulsive. I need his focus to stay on basketball."

"Don't worry. This time, I've taken extra precautions. The shipment is secure. Lincoln won't be involved. He won't even know about it."

I breathed a sigh of relief. "Good. I appreciate that. We can't afford any slip-ups."

"I'm aware. This shipment of drugs is invaluable. Our buyers—well, they're not the most patient bunch of mothafuckas."

"Agreed."

"Like I said, I've got everything under control. The crates are discreetly labeled, and the paperwork is impeccable. No room for misunderstandings this time."

"Good. I was tired of losing sleep over this shit. Let's keep it that way—quiet, efficient, and no fuckin' family entanglements."

"Absolutely, Brains. I've got eyes on every detail. It's guaranteed smooth sailing ahead, my friend."

I ended the call feeling relieved yet cautious. Vincent's assurances echoed in my mind as I contemplated the delicate dance of secrecy and precision—extra precautions, secrecy, and the promise that Lincoln wouldn't catch a whiff of our operation.

I sat by the window in my study, grappling with the other tangled emotions that trapped me as the spring shower tapped a melancholy rhythm. My wisdom had whispered to my conscience, and I'd released my little dove like a fragile moth fluttering away from a dying flame. My fingers traced the lines on my face as I closed my eyes, seeking solace in the rain's soft cadence. The curves of her body would forever remain imprinted in the margins of my memory. My dick throbbed, a bittersweet ache, as I thought about our private lessons in longing.

Each recollection was dipped in her sweet sepia tones and melodic moans—the way she slightly closed her eyes when I recited poetry as if the world narrowed to just us two. Underneath her desk, her legs were wide with wonder, absorbing her touch as she secretly pleasured herself.

Female students had been throwing themselves at my feet for years, and from time to time, I'd dabble in their whirlwind of youth. But as the years rolled by, I yearned for simplicity, Cassandra's quiet embrace, and the familiar warmth of shared mornings by the beach. I knew the boundaries set by my vows, the weight of years spent with my wife, and our history woven into the grooves of my most cherished memories. Our love was as seasoned as aged wine while my infatuation for Ava danced around my mind like a fleeting firefly. Ava was a storm I hadn't prepared for and a forbidden sonnet I dared no longer recite. She deserved more than stolen kisses, and the limitations entangling herself with me would bring. I was an ancient oak whose roots were already anchored deep in another woman's soil.

My thoughts settled on Cassandra. I knew I had to mend the pieces of our relationship that had unraveled over the years. In the meantime, I needed to pacify her to ease the tremors of suspicion that secretly rattled her soul. She hadn't said a word to me, but I could tell by how she looked at me. Once warm and trusting, her eyes now held a guarded skepticism whenever I entered the room. I left my study to find her, searching every room on the main level until I located her in the sunroom off the kitchen. I approached her cautiously like a tightrope walker inching across a narrow wire.

"Baby, you got a minute? I want to have a serious conversation."

Her eyes bore into mine with a lifetime of intel etched in her amber-colored orbs. "About?"

"Me leaving the business for good."

Her unyielding gaze remained fixed on me. "We've had this conversation a million times, Augustine. What makes this one different?"

"Because, this time, I'm serious," I insisted. "I'm handing things over to Vincent. He's reliable. Responsible. He can handle it."

Cassandra's silence hung in the room, a weighty verdict. She'd been riding in the passenger seat for almost two decades and had seen the darkness that clung to our lives, the murky waters of the game. In some ways, she'd become just as accustomed to death and bloody money as I had. But I was ready to leave it all behind and write a new chapter of redemption and renewal with her by my side.

"If you're serious this time and Vincent truly takes the reins, then what?"

"I want to sell the house and buy a house on the water."

She raised an eyebrow. "Sell the house? What about my career, Augustine?"

"You can practice anywhere, Cass. Besides, Lincoln's grown. He's got one more year in college. He's not coming back home to us. He's looking ahead, and we should be, too. Don't you want to wake up on the beach every morning?"

"Yes, of course. But—"

I cut her off. "We've always said our forever home would be right on the water. It'll be where we'd watch our grandchildren grow and live out our golden years."

"I know, Augustine. That's why we still have our beach house. We rarely visit there anymore, and now suddenly you want an entire house on the water?"

"Our forever home will be bigger and better than the beach house, Cass. Imagine waking up every morning to the soft glow of the sunrise, its warm rays dancing across the beautiful blue waves. And at night, the roaring sound of the ocean lulling us to sleep. It'll be like our own private paradise. A little piece of heaven where we can sip our morning coffee on the deck or with our toes in the sand."

She chuckled. "Since when do you like your toes in the sand?"

I shrugged. "It's growing on me."

She sighed, her resolve crumbling. "Is that the only part of your grand exit plan?"

I reached for her hand, the distance between us collapsing. "The beach house? It's only the beginning, baby."

Cassandra's gaze continued to soften. "Augustine, we've built so many memories here. Our home is cozy, familiar..." she acknowledged, letting her voice trail off as her fingers traced the edge of her teacup. "Selling our home is a big decision."

"Memories aren't tied to walls or roofs. And think about all the new memories we'll create there, the laughter echoing through the beach house, our grandchildren building sandcastles, and lazy afternoons reading by the water."

"It does sound blissful. But what about the practical things? Our neighbors, the convenience of being close to things."

"Fuck these neighbors, Cass. We'll thrive wherever we go, baby. We always do."

The path ahead was unknown, but I had made my choice. I'd vowed to leave the game and steer our ship toward calmer shores. I wasn't going back on that for anybody. The room held its breath as I stood by the couch, waiting for Cassandra's verdict.

"It's not a yes, but it's not a no. Show me some appealing listings, and *maybe* we can consider moving."

I smiled. "Thank you. Now that we've gotten that out of the way, we can get to the fun part."

"Fun part?" she questioned.

I extended my hand to hers. "My lady."

She arched an inquisitive brow as she slowly rose to her feet and placed her hand in mine. "What do you have going on inside that mind of yours now, Augustine?"

"Follow me."

I led her down the hall and back into my study, where an oversized wall map of the world adorned the far wall. There were pins in all the locations we'd traveled to, ranging from Greece to the Champagne region of France.

"Pick a place," I urged, my voice a gentle breeze as I aimed my index finger at the map. "Anywhere on this map. Wherever you want to go, and I'll make the arrangements."

"What?"

"You heard me, Mrs. Hill. Pick a place."

"What's the occasion?"

"You and me, baby. We're the occasion."

She stepped up to the map and hesitated, her fingertip tracing the contours of continents. And then, her finger landed on a familiar city with promises of romance and long Parisian nights in the city beneath the moonlight.

"Paris," she answered, her voice soft as rose petals brushing against skin. "Take me back to Paris."

My heart swelled with a mixture of joy and nostalgia. It was the place where she said yes to becoming my wife.

I stepped closer to her. "Paris it is," I declared, eyes locking onto hers. "Je t'aime," I murmured, the words a delicate dance on my tongue. "I love you."

Cass smiled, her lips curving like the arc of a crescent moon. "Je t'aime plus," she replied, her fingers brushing against mine. "I love you more."

THE STEPSON

The gym echoed with the cadenced bounce of basketballs as the team wrapped up practice. My sneakers squeaked against the polished floor as I stepped out of the gym and into the cool evening air. I was sweat-soaked and felt my adrenaline still pumping when I spotted Jemal leaning against the brick wall, waiting patiently.

"Yo, Linc!" he grinned, pushing off the wall. "Practice was brutal, huh?"

I nodded, wiping my face with a towel. "Yeah, Coach is relentless. But it's what we signed up for," I answered, shrugging it off.

We fell into step, walking across campus toward my dorm. Jemal had been my homie since our freshman year at WBU. He was a lanky point guard with hoop dreams as high as the stadium rafters. We were the only two freshman starters in our first year. Jemal was on fire, dazzling the fans with his crossovers and sinking three-pointers like clockwork. But sophomore year brought a cruel twist. His game and his grades slipped, too. The coach's patience wore thin, and Jemal's once bright basketball career faded to nothing.

We reached my dorm room, and I fumbled with the key. Inside, the room was cramped, with posters of basketball legends covering the walls. I tossed my gym bag onto the bed and headed for the shower. As the water cascaded over me, my mind wandered to the unopened letter from my father on my desk. The last one was filled with ink-stained pleas for money to get a lawyer for an appeal of his probation denial, and I wasn't trying to hear any of that shit.

I emerged from the bathroom wearing a fresh tee and basketball shorts. I entered my room and saw Jemal sitting cross-legged on the bed, holding the unopened letter. *Fuck.* His expression was serious, eyes scanning the faded ink.

"What's this?" he asked, tapping the paper. "Who the fuck you know in prison?"

I dashed over and snatched it from his hand, crumpling it in my fist. "Mind your fuckin' business, nigga."

"No need to get sensitive."

My jaw tightened before my confession spilled from my lips. "It's my old man."

"Your old man?" he quizzed, confusion imprinted in his brow.

"My biological father."

His brows heightened. "Hold up. Professor H ain't your father?"

"Not by blood."

Jemal raised an eyebrow. "Oh shit."

I hesitated, then sank onto the bed beside him. "Yeah. We reconnected a while back, and I don't know. It's been cool getting to know him, I guess. But then he started asking for money and shit."

"For what? His books?"

"A lawyer for an appeal."

Jemal studied me. "How you feel about that, Linc? Deep down?"

My chest tightened. "Angry. Confused. Part of me wants to do it. But another part wonders if I should help."

"You're not responsible for that nigga's choices. You got your own life to think about."

"He's behind bars, but it's like he's draining my soul from there."

"Yeah, well, my old man's not in prison, but he might as well be. Cancer's eating him alive. The doctors say there's an experimental trial that could save him, but it costs a fortune. We're already drowning in medical bills."

I sighed. We were both desperate for cash for different reasons. "Damn."

"Imagine watching your father fade away, and there wasn't a damn thing you could do about it."

"Fuck it. Maybe we're both screwed."

A cynical chuckle slipped past his lips. "Screwed together."

———

The next day, Ava and I strolled across the cobblestone pathway on campus, hand in hand, our footsteps trekking in sync as we headed toward my campus apartment.

"Lincoln," she said, her voice soft, "I've been thinking. Can we visit your family's beach house this weekend?"

I glanced at her as my heart skipped a beat. I immediately thought about the safe at the beach house. "Why?" I asked, curious.

She hesitated to respond, then looked out toward the distant horizon. "The waves," she answered. "I don't know. I can't explain it."

"Just try."

Ava's chest deflated with a hard sigh. "It's almost like they've been... calling me. I need to be there, baby. To clear my mind."

"All right," I replied. "I'll make the arrangements. We'll go back this weekend."

A bright smile spread across her face. "Really?"

I dipped my chin. "Yeah. I'll call my mom when I get back to my room. It shouldn't be a problem."

She tossed her arms around my neck and kissed my cheek. "Thank you, baby. I'm so excited. I can't wait to feel the breeze through my hair. I can practically feel the sand between my toes already."

"I bet you'll be daydreaming about it nonstop for the rest of the week."

She laughed. "Hell yeah! The sun, the waves, the lazy afternoons... it's going to be perfect."

I wrapped my arm around Ava's waist. "And we'll have the whole weekend to ourselves. What do you want to do while we're there?"

"Hmm, let's see. Well, first things first, I want to wake up early Saturday morning and catch the sunrise."

"Okay. Sunrise it is. And then?"

Her perfectly arched brows shot toward her hairline. "Oh! And we should build a sandcastle! And then later that evening, maybe we can have a bonfire on the beach. We can roast marshmallows and watch the stars. You know, real cute white people shit," she explained with a chuckle. "It's going to be so romantic."

I laughed. "Damn, now you got me excited. I can't wait for this weekend."

"Me neither. It's going to be unforgettable."

We continued walking toward my student apartment as Ava talked about our upcoming weekend. But little did she know that if I had it my way, a darker tale would unfold.

———

I sat at my desk, phone in hand, before dialing my mother. I explained that Ava and I needed a quick weekend escape and asked for the keys to the beach house. She agreed, her familiar voice warm and understanding. Then, I texted Ava to let her know the good news.

Me: *Arrangements made. We leave on Friday.*

Ava: *OMG. I'm so excited! I can't wait!*

I paced the floor in my cramped dorm room as I exited our message thread and dialed Jemal's number. Ever since Ava had brought up returning to the beach house, an insidious plan had taken root inside my mind. And since Jemal had always had a knack for trouble, I knew he was the only one I could share it with.

"What's up?" Jemal's baritone voice crackled through the line.

"Where are you at right now?" I asked, cutting straight to the chase.

"I'm around. Why?"

"How soon can you get to campus?"

"I'm already here. Wassup?"

"My girl and I are going back to the beach house this weekend," I informed him, my voice low. "It's time to put our play into action."

Jemal's laughter echoed. "You've got my attention."

"How soon can you meet me?"

"Shit, I can be on the way to you right now."

"Nah. Don't come here. I don't wanna risk one of my roommates comin' in. I'll meet you near the old oak tree beside the dining hall."

"Say less. I'm on the way."

———

The moon hung like a silver coin as Jemal and I met near the old oak tree fifteen minutes later.

"So, wassup, nigga? What's the play?" Jemal queried, rubbing his hands together.

"You remember the safe I told you about inside the beach house?" I whispered to him.

"Yeah."

"I think we should stage a break-in."

His brows heightened. "Word?"

"Yeah. I'll leave the door unlocked since I'll already be there with her. Then you break in, cause a scene, scare us a bit, and ask where the safe is. I'll open it, and then you take shit, Jemal. Then we flip the bricks and split the profit."

Jemal's eyes gleamed. "That sounds like a risky move, my friend. But if we pull it off, we'll be fuckin' legends."

"So, are you in?" I challenged as our shadows danced around us as we conspired in the darkness.

A sinister smirk slithered up one side of his mouth. "Hell yeah, I'm in."

I saw the excitement across Jemal's face. His ass thrived on adrenaline. The thrill of danger and the taste of rebellion electrified him. I knew he was the perfect person to stage the robbery with because at the first mention of the beach house's safe, he was ready to dance with fate, consequences be damned.

"You still got that DC connect you told me about?" I asked.

He nodded. "Yeah. I do."

"You think you can get the bricks off to him?"

"Hell yeah. And shit, if we play our cards right, we can take that money and re-up. We'll have our own organization up and running in no time."

My heart raced as I contemplated the risk. I felt the weight of betrayal toward my family and Ava. Yet, my mind had been made. The allure of creating my own wealth and the promise of escape fueled me. I was willing to gamble everything for a chance at a different life, even if it meant shredding our fabric of trust.

"Aight, bet," I answered as we clasped hands, sealing our pact.

Jemal's plan sounded like everything I wanted to hear. All I ever wanted to do was prove myself to my father. I had been dreaming about taking over his business for years. And if he didn't want to hand me the keys to his kingdom, I'd build my own.

———

Friday arrived, and Ava and I tossed our bags in the trunk in the mid-afternoon and headed to the beach house. As the wheels turned, our conversation flowed like the winding road leading us to our destination.

Ava gazed out at the passing landscape. "Can you believe I'm almost done with college? It feels like I blinked, and now it's graduation season."

I chuckled. "Yeah, time flies when you're cramming for finals and surviving on Ramen noodles. But hey, you made it, baby."

I sighed. "Yeah, I did. And now what? My sisters and parents call me every five seconds to talk about job offers, grad school, and adulting. It's overwhelming. Sometimes, I feel like I'm drowning in expectations—my own and everyone else's. That's why I needed to be back at the beach."

"I'm glad I could make this happen for you then," I responded as I reached for her hand.

She gently slid her hand away from mine while keeping her gaze fixated out of the window. "Linc, do you ever wonder about our future? Like, what happens to us post-graduation?"

"What do you mean?"

"You know, like... us sticking together."

"I've made it clear I want to be with you, Ava. And after I graduate, we could start our lives together and build something lasting like what my parents have."

She finally twisted her neck to face me. "Listen, Lincoln, I've spent the last four years studying and preparing. And now, it's like I'm stepping into this vast unknown. I don't know what I want or where I want to work. Somedays, I think I wanna go straight to grad school. Then, other days, I want to spend a year traveling the world. The only thing I do know is that I can't tie myself down right now."

"Ava, baby, I get it. But what if we're meant to be? What if our dreams align somehow? I see a future with you, building a home, and maybe raising a family someday."

She shook her head in frustration. "Lincoln, we're still so young! We can't plan our whole lives now. I want to explore, take risks, and *not* settle. I don't want to wake up one day and realize I missed out on something big."

I gripped the steering wheel tighter. All I'd been trying to do was do things that brought us closer together, yet Ava was steadily trying to pull us apart. "But what if the big thing is us? What if we're the adventure? Ava, I-I love you. Shit, if I'm being sincere, I've loved you since that poetry slam my sophomore year when you recited your heart out."

Her breath hitched. "You remember that?"

"I remember everything about you, baby."

She sighed. "I just feel like I'm at a crossroads and need to choose my path. I can't promise you forever."

"Forever scares you, huh?"

"It's bigger than that. I don't want to hurt you, Linc."

"I'm a grown-ass man. I can handle myself. Let me decide when I've had too much."

Ava reached out for my hand with a fractured smile. "Okay, then. You always find a way to calm my storms, baby."

I smiled. "I'm your man. It's my job to navigate whatever waves come our way. No matter what, I'll keep coming back."

———

I pulled up to the beach house a half hour later. The familiar summer getaway stood weathered but welcoming. I unlocked the door, and the scent of the ocean waves enveloped us. Ava stepped onto the deck, her brown orbs drawn to the restless waves. I pulled her body close to mine, our heartbeats in sync with the rising tide.

"I'm sorry you've been so stressed," I said, kissing her forehead.

Her thin fingers traced the wooden railing. "My sister told me it will pass. I'm still waiting."

A breath eased out as I fished my phone out of my pocket. The screen illuminated with unanswered messages to Jemal. *Why the fuck isn't this nigga answering my texts?*

"Everything okay?" Ava inquired.

"Mmhm. I'll be back. I'm going to bring our bags inside from the car."

After bringing the bags inside, I paced the bedroom as Jemal's silence gnawed at my insides like an endless tide. As the darkness settled, the beach house seemed to hold its breath. I hadn't heard from him in hours and wondered if he'd decided to call the whole thing off without informing me. I'd sent him the address and told him I'd left the door unlocked.

"Shit," I hissed as the phone rang against my ear. "Pick up the fuckin' phone, Jemal."

You've reached Jemal Ahmed. I can't come to the phone right now.
Click

I tried to settle my nerves before heading back downstairs to find Ava. When I finally returned outside, I found her sitting on the balcony, her mahogany legs dangling over the railing. She sipped from a glass of chilled white wine with her eyes closed as if absorbing the waves' power. I stepped onto the balcony, the wooden planks cool beneath my bare feet. I leaned against the railing, watching her. She was the picture of serenity, a visible difference from the restless energy inside me. Her long eyelashes fluttered open seconds later, and she smiled at me. It was the kind of smile that made my heart skip a beat.

"Join me, handsome," she insisted, patting the space beside her on the cushioned lounge chair. "The view is incredible."

I hesitated, torn between the ocean's calming allure and the weight of my secret. I stole a quick glance at Ava, wondering how she'd react when the shadows came alive when the line between reality and staged chaos blurred.

"Hey, uh, I've been thinking about tonight."

Her eyes sparkled with curiosity. "What about it?"

I took a deep breath. "I want it to be special. Intimate. Y'know, just us."

Ava's smile widened. "You're full of surprises."

I leaned in, brushing my lips against her temple. "I'm about to go take a shower. Promise me you'll come in soon and stay inside for the rest of the night."

She raised an eyebrow. "Stay inside? Why? What's going on?"

I glanced back at the beach house. My heart raced from the impending surprise and the knowledge that I'd left the door unlocked, a deliberate invitation for Jemal to breach our private sanctuary. "Because I want you all to myself tonight. I plan to fuck you all over this beach house."

Ava shot me an alluring gaze before pecking my lips and returning to watching the waves kiss the shore. "Mmm. Don't tempt me with a good time."

I smirked before playfully slapping her ass. "I'll be back."

I stepped away from her and trekked back inside. As much as I wanted to, I couldn't get Jemal off my mind. I clenched my teeth, torn between anger and loyalty. I heard my father's voice inside my head saying, "*Broken promises sink ships, son.*" I paced the bathroom, phone still in hand, waiting for Jemal's next move. My jaw tightened as I redialed his number. That time, it went straight to voicemail. The shower continued to run, drowning out my rage as I slammed my fist against the wall. We were on the brink of success, and his ass was playing games. He was jeopardizing everything.

My phone vibrated, and I jumped, nearly dropping it. "Jemal, where are you?" I answered, frustrated. "We had a fuckin' deal! You can't bail on me now, nigga!"

"Don't worry about it, nigga. I got this."

"Where are you? Are you close?" I probed before the line went dead. "Fuck!" I hissed.

I had to hurry up and shower to get back to Ava. She had no idea that our weekend escape would turn into a nightmare. The minute I stepped out of the shower, I heard Ava scream. I quickly pulled on my basketball shorts and raced downstairs. I paused when I saw Ava standing in the middle of the living room floor with her trembling hands in the air. Instantly, the tranquility of the beach house had shattered like fragile seashells, replaced by the harsh reality of Jemal's staged intrusion. The air thickened with tension as my pulse raced in sync with the crashing waves outside. Jemal stood there, his face covered in a black mask. His eyes were cold and desperate. The gun in his hand gleamed under the dim light. Adrenaline surged through my veins. We'd *never* talked about guns. My eyes darted over to the loose hinge on the door. He'd kicked it open. I'd seen movies and heard stories, but this shit was too real for TV, a true nightmare woven into reality.

"Where's the safe, mothafucka?" He drilled me as soon as my foot hit the bottom step.

His raspy voice was an eerie symphony of greed and desperation. He aimed the gun at me, and I stumbled backward, mind racing. Ava clung to the arm of the sofa, her brown eyes wide with terror.

"W-we don't h-have a safe," I stammered. "Please, just take whatever else you want."

Jemal's eyes narrowed. "Don't lie to me, nigga." He gestured toward Ava. "She knows something. I can tell."

Ava's breaths came in shallow gasps. Her legs trembled as she backed away, her gaze darting between me and the masked intruder. Her desperate eyes searched mine, unaware of my mask of fake innocence during the orchestrated chaos. Before either of us could react, Jemal lunged at her and pressed the cold metal of his gun against her temple.

"Oh my God, please don't shoot me! T-there is a s-safe!" she screamed. "It's over there, in the d-dining room b-behind the p-picture!"

"She just told you where it was! Now leave her the fuck alone!" I roared, voice cracking.

I'd never seen that side of Jemal before. It was as if something inside him had flipped.

"Show me where it's at then, bitch," he demanded.

"P-please. We're just a normal couple. We don't even k-know the code to—hold up," she paused, recognizing Jemal's voice. "J—Jemal? Is... is that you?"

She let her sentence trail off before looking at Jemal and then back at me. Ava didn't hesitate. She lunged toward the balcony, her bare feet slipping on the polished floor. A loud gunshot echoed through the room, and my heart stopped. Ava didn't fall; she stumbled, her head colliding with the corner of the table. Darkness swallowed her, and I watched her crumple to the floor.

"Fuck! What the fuck did she have to go and make a move for?" Jemal screamed, pacing the floor as he rested his hands on his head. I stood frozen to the ground, torn between pursuing Ava and Jemal. He turned to me, aiming the gun in my direction. "Open the safe!" he barked at me. "Now, nigga!"

"It wasn't supposed to happen like this, Jemal! What the fuck are you doing, nigga?"

"I said open the fuckin' safe!" he roared, still aiming the gun straight at my head.

My brow creased. "Nigga, what are you on right now? You buggin'!"

Instead of responding, he swung his head from left to right. "I ain't gon' ask your ass again."

"W-what the f-fuck?"

My hands shook as I led the way to the dining room, where the safe was hidden behind a painting, just as we all knew. I fumbled with the combination, sweat dripping down my forehead. The correct numbers finally aligned, and the safe clicked open.

But before I could react, Jemal struck me, sending a hard blow to the back of my head. There was an excruciating burst of pain before everything went black. The room spun like a Ferris wheel before I collapsed. The last thing I heard was Jemal's voice.

"Good lookin' out, mothafucka."

———

My eyes cracked open as I lay crumpled in the fetal position on the dining room floor. The room spun around me like a broken carousel. The pain at the back of my skull pulsed in rhythm with my lulled heartbeat. I tried to move, but my limbs refused to obey. The room tilted as minutes stretched into an eternity. My vision narrowed to a pinprick before my lids shut again. My thoughts were a jumble of memories—from my first kiss with Ava to the sound of the safe door creaking open, the scent of her dark hair, and Jemal's triumphant mutter. The beach house walls closed in as Ava's face lingered heavily on my mind, a desperate prayer for her safety once I recalled more of what happened before I blacked out.

I continued to regain consciousness. My head throbbed, and the taste of copper lingered on my tongue. The dim light filtering through my eyelids revealed a messy room—the overturned coffee table, the empty safe, and the lingering scent of fear—all the aftermath of the violent intrusion. My heart raced as I stumbled to my feet. The realization hit me like a punch to the gut: the money, jewelry, and drugs were gone, and Ava was missing. Jemal had taken her, too. Panic surged through my veins, and I clutched the edge of the dining room table for support. What kind of fucked up shit was Jemal on?

I imagined Ava's face, how she'd look when she woke up, how afraid she'd be. I prayed she was safe and that Jemal didn't take things to the point of no return. My thoughts galloped nonstop. I had no experience with kidnappings, no secret stash of weapons, and no fuckin' idea where to start. My parents were hours away, but I had no choice. I needed help. My fingers twitched, seeking the phone in my pocket. Just as I was about to dial my father's number, the phone rang. The screen displayed an unfamiliar local number. I hesitated, then answered.

My voice cracked as I spoke, "Who is this?"

A female responded, "Lincoln... you're looking for Ava, aren't you?" Her familiar yet unplaceable voice sent a chill down my spine. "We have her. She's alive—for now."

My anger flared. "We? Bitch, where is she, and where the fuck is Jemal? Put his ass on the fuckin' phone! I wanna speak to him right now!"

"Calm the fuck down, Lincoln. My brother told me all about your plan."

I paused. "*Your brother*? Hold up, is this Karina!" I snapped, gripping the phone tighter. "Are you two mothafuckas trying to play me?"

Jemal had confided in me in the past about his father's failing health. I knew their family was drowning in debt, owing medical bill to collectors who played by their own rules. The doctors had given him six months to live without the treatment. Now, in some ways, the clock was ticking for all of us.

Her voice chuckled, devoid of any humanity. "You have something we want."

The silence stretched, and my mind raced. *How much will it cost to buy Ava's life?* "Jemal took everything from the fuckin' safe and knocked my ass out, Karina! I don't have anything to give!"

"But your father does. Those were his bricks Jemal stole, *right*?"

"Listen to me, Karina. You don't wanna fuck with my father. Me and your brother had a deal. He went rogue, and now your ass needs to help me get Ava and all the extra shit he stole back before my father finds out and kills us all!"

"You're not the one calling the shots anymore, Lincoln. In all honesty, you never were. I already told you I know all about the staged robbery you cooked up with my brother. Y'know, the dirty little secret you've kept hidden from everyone, including little Miss Ava and dear old dad. So, if you want her back and you wanna keep your little secret between us, you'll do exactly as I say."

My chest heaved as I pushed out an explosive sigh. "You better not hurt a hair on her fuckin' head, Karina! What the fuck do you want?"

She cackled. "If you knew what I knew, you wouldn't be worried about that two-dollar ho. Now listen the fuck up. You have twenty-four hours to get me half a million dollars. Follow my instructions precisely, or this bitch dies, and your parents find out you were the one behind the robbery. And remember, Lincoln, silence is your currency now."

The line went dead, leaving me trembling with rage and fear. I sank back down to the floor, staring at the phone. Guilt gnawed at me. Exposure would mean being exiled from my family or worse. Ava's life hung in the balance, and I had no choice but to play Karina and Jemal's twisted game.

The TA

My reckless brother had dragged us into one hell of a mess. The way he'd explained everything to me, the heist was supposed to be a simple job—a quick in-and-out, no complications. But Jemal's impulsive streak had turned it into a twisted game of cat and mouse. Jemal and I were held up in the dimly lit basement of an old building on campus near the library. I'd stumbled upon the hidden spot my sophomore year and visited it often to clear my mind. I'd even met Cassandra there a few dozen times for private rendezvous. But this time, I found myself in a tangled mess of secrets and betrayal with a hostage who had no idea what trouble she'd encountered.

"You absolute idiot!" I berated Jemal as soon as I ended the call with Lincoln. "We had a perfect plan, and you just had to go all cowboy on us, didn't you? Taking a fucking hostage? Seriously?"

"Chill, Kit Kat."

"No! Why the fuck would you do this? You were just supposed to get the cash and hold the theatrics!"

"I'm willing to extort whoever and do whatever if it means it gets our father in that fuckin' trial. I thought you and I were on the same type of time, sis."

"I was, but—"

He cut me off. "No buts! The window is closing soon, right? You know what the fuck we gotta do."

"Yeah, only now we've got a live hostage in your trunk, and I'm pretty sure she's not enjoying the ride!"

"Right now, I've got enough to pay those mothafuckas back that I owe *and* enough to get Dad into the trial. Once we get the money from Lincoln's parents, we will be set for life. No more debt, Kit Kat. No more struggles. You just gotta hold it down for me a little while longer."

I sighed. "Is she dead?"

"No. I ain't kill the bitch. I'm not stupid. I didn't hurt her. Just tied her up a bit."

I scoffed while pacing the floor. "Yeah, well, I'm not so fuckin' sure about that, nigga. But we're in too deep to quit now. What's the next move in your brilliant plan, huh?"

Jemal shot me a cold glare. "Let's get her out of the damn trunk first, and then I can take it from there."

I eased out a breath. "Fine. And, Jemal, next time, stick to the fuckin' plan. No more hostages!" I yelled.

With a reluctant nod, he followed me outside. He opened the trunk, revealing Ava's crumpled unconscious body inside. There was dried blood caked up on the side of her forehead.

"I thought you said she wasn't hurt!" I fussed.

"I said she wasn't dead, and I didn't hurt her. She tried to run and ended up falling and hitting her head. After she blacked out, I made the split decision to bring her along for collateral."

Once we'd gotten back inside with Ava in tow, I stood back and watched Jemal dial Lincoln's number. The phone rang twice before Lincoln picked up, and Jemal put the call on speakerphone.

"Hello?" Lincoln answered frantically. "Jemal?"

"Linc," Jemal whispered. "It's me."

"Where the fuck are you?"

"Listen carefully. I'm in deep trouble. My sister, Karina, she's gone crazy. She made me flip on you, nigga. She's the one who told me to take Ava, and I'm pretty sure she's planning to kill her, nigga!"

"How do I know I can trust you?" Lincoln quizzed.

"Because I just told you everything, nigga! You gotta believe me! I'll hold her off as long as I can, but you need to get here."

"Where are you?"

"I'll text you the address. Get here ASAP," Jemal advised before abruptly ending the call.

My brow creased as I stood with tightly folded arms across my chest. "What the fuck was that about? Why the fuck would you throw me under the bus like that?" I hissed.

Jemal snapped his neck in my direction. "Would you chill the fuck out? He's on his way, ain't he? And when he gets here, we'll turn this shit up a notch to make sure we get what we need."

"You better know what you're doing."

"I *always* know what I'm doing, sis."

I sighed briefly as my thoughts transferred to Lincoln before settling on his mother. My weekly sessions with Cassandra had become my lifeline. Then, out of nowhere, I got a call from her office receptionist saying I'd been reassigned to a new therapist. Cassandra had acted on her word and passed me off like a baton. I thought therapy was supposed to be a safe space, but it felt more like I was being shuffled around like unnecessary paperwork.

Initially, I grappled with the shock of betrayal. I wondered if she ever truly understood my pain, the way my anxiety clenched my chest, leaving me breathless. The way my depression swallowed me whole some days like a black hole. My whirlwind of emotions swirled with betrayal, anger, and hurt. Cassandra, the person I trusted, had shattered our bond, leaving me to question everything I believed about our connection. I should've stuck to my guns and left her that night at the diner. I never should've gotten in her car and let her butter me up at that hotel. As reality continued to sink in, anger flared. I was wronged. Revenge consumed my thoughts as I replayed memories, scrutinizing every detail for clues. My mind became a war room, my asylum for vengeful thoughts. I became obsessed with exposing Cassandra's deceit. I had a primal urge to make her hurt as deeply as I did. Her ass needed to feel the weight of her actions. And when the money came, I'd reveal the truth.

Lincoln texted Jemal's phone an hour and a half later, notifying us of his arrival. He pushed open the door, scanning the room. As soon as his frantic gaze landed on Ava sitting tied up in a corner, his eyes darted around, searching for my brother. But before he could call out, Jemal and I fully stepped out of the shadows, me holding a gun and Jemal with a baseball bat in hand.

Lincoln jumped. "Jemal, what the hell is—"

"Sorry, nigga. No time for explanations," Jemal told him while twisting the bat.

Whack! The bat connected with Lincoln's temple, and he immediately dropped to the floor.

We peered over his still body. "Nice swing, little brother," I complimented him.

Jemal panted. "Thanks. Now help me tie his ass up. We need to figure out our next move before he wakes up."

My pulse raced, adrenaline pumping fiercely through my veins. I'd always been the cautious one, the planner, the shadow behind the scenes. But now? I reveled in the taste of power. Whenever I glanced at Ava or Lincoln's unconscious, blood-stained faces, I couldn't help but smirk. We had the upper hand for the first time, holding the power of life and death in our grasp. I glanced at my brother, who was busy tying up his unconscious friend. His loyalty to our family had been unwavering, even amidst the chaos.

"Open the bag," I instructed Jemal. "I wanna see everything you got from the safe."

Jemal laughed while rubbing his palms together. "I cleaned that bitch out. I'm tellin' you, sis, it's up from here on out!"

We walked over to a table, and he laid out everything in front of us. There were twelve stacks of cash, diamonds winking in the dim light, and four neatly wrapped bricks of pure cocaine. My fingers itched to touch them, to feel the weight of our newfound fortune in the palm of my hand. Jemal and I were sitting on top of the world. Maybe we'd do more than survive this. Perhaps we'd become legends, the Ahmed siblings who outwitted fate. But one thing was sure: I would savor every drop of our moment. The taste of power and the rush of danger was intoxicating. For the first time, I felt like a puppeteer pulling the strings. And it felt damn good.

———

After a while, Lincoln and Ava started to come to, groaning in pain. Both of them were tied up, gagged, and disoriented. Lincoln's eyes darted around, taking in the dimly lit room. And there we were, standing over them like vultures. My icy gaze bore into his as my lips twisted in a wicked smile.

I leaned into Lincoln while holding up his phone to his face to unlock it. "Rise and shine, sleepyhead. It's time to call your daddy."

His eyes widened as he tried to speak, but the gag muffled his words.

"It's time to pay up. When he answers, tell him if he doesn't wire us half a million, his precious son won't see the light of day. Oh, and neither will his little girlfriend. Isn't that right, *Little Dove*?"

My eyes bore into Ava's, daring her to defy me by making a sound. Her fearful gaze widened as she broke contact with me to look at Lincoln. I signaled to Jemal to remove his gag so he could speak freely.

"W-what? What are you talking about?" Lincoln inquired.

I smirked. "You see, Lincoln, I'm playing a different game, one with much higher stakes. And your daddy's my golden ticket."

"Tell me what you mean by what you said!"

"Let's make the call and ask him, shall we?" Ava continued to whimper, trying to form audible sentences through her gag. "Or do you wanna be the one to break the news to him?" I asked her.

She looked as if she were about to shit herself. Neither of them had been on this side of the equation before.

"Ask Daddy for the money, and I'll keep your secrets. So, what'll it be?" I quizzed, with the foresight that calling Lincoln's father was his only way out.

THE PROFESSOR

The departure lounge at the airport in Seven Pines buzzed with anticipation—the scent of freshly brewed coffee mixed with the nervous energy of travelers. Cass and I stood side by side with our hands tightly clasped. Our flight to Paris was scheduled to take off in less than an hour. The Eiffel Tower, the Seine River, and the promise of rekindled romance awaited us. My phone vibrated in my pocket. I pulled it out and glanced at the caller ID to see Lincoln's name.

"Who is it, baby?" Cass inquired, noticing the hesitation carved into my expression.

"Lincoln. Isn't he supposed to be at the beach house this weekend?"

"Yeah, with his girlfriend," she confirmed.

"Then why is he calling?"

Cass shrugged lazily. "I don't know. Maybe they got locked out or something. Answer it and see."

I pressed accept before nestling the phone against my ear. "What do you need, son?"

"D-dad! Dad, help! I need your help!" Lincoln called out, voice frantic.

My heart skipped a beat as I stood and quickly stepped away from the crowd. "Lincoln! Son? What's wrong?"

"They're gonna kill us both if you don't give them what they ask for! Please help us, Dad!" he cried through the receiver.

I heard a muffled sound before another distorted voice echoed through the line. "We have your son *and* his girlfriend. They're alive, *for now.*"

My mind raced. *How could this happen?* "Who are you, and what do you want?"

"Half a million dollars in cash," the voice replied. "I'll send an address. No police. No tricks. You have twenty-four hours, or they both die."

My breath caught. The closer I got to getting out of the game for good, the more I kept getting sucked back in. I didn't want any more blood on my hands, but I would do what I had to do for my family. I would burn all of Potomac Falls to the fucking ground if I had to. Cass's eyes met mine from across the bustling terminal. She instantly sensed my distress and hurried over.

"Augustine, what's wrong?" she whispered, her eyes wide.

"We need to go," I confirmed.

Her brows creased. "What? Why? Is Lincoln okay? What did he say on the phone?"

I sighed before relaying the call as discreetly as possible, my voice barely audible. All the melanin in Cassandra's face seemed to flush right out. "You know we can't involve the police, or they'll kill them both."

Cass's gaze hardened as desperation clawed at her chest. "But how can we get that much cash in twenty-four hours?"

I clenched my jaw. "We have no choice. We play by their rules. Our son's life is at stake."

We quickly canceled our flight and headed back to the parking garage. When we got to the car, our dreams of Paris had faded like mist. The Eiffel Tower would have to wait. Instead, we drove through the rain-soaked streets of Seven Pines, desperate to cross over the bridge and get back to Potomac Falls. My hand gripped the steering wheel as I dialed Vinny's number. Cass scrolled through her phone, moving money around to appease the kidnappers' demands.

THE WIFE

Finding out there was a ransom on my son's head shook me to the core. Not only was I afraid for his life, but I was also afraid the kidnapper's hefty financial request would lead my husband to discover I'd been siphoning money bit by bit to fund the secret dinners and stolen moments in hotels with Karina. For the first time, the car felt smaller and airless, as if the walls were closing in on me. I clutched the phone, its cold plastic digging into my palm as I tried to move money around to cover my tracks. Panic and disbelief intertwined in my gut like a knot. No matter how hard I tried, I couldn't shake the sinister feeling that sliced through my composure. I'd spent months—no, over a year—skimming money from our accounts.

Augustine and I were supposed to be leaving to reignite the passion in one of the most romantic places on earth, Paris. It brought me joy to know we both wanted to put the focus back on saving our marriage. Our bags were packed, filled with the dresses I'd bought for Paris and the lingerie meant to ignite our spark. But passion was a double-edged sword, and Karina's touch still burned on my skin. She was the one who knew every curve of my skin and the taste of my lies. She was the reason my marriage would soon crumble like a fragile pastry. I couldn't lose my son. But I couldn't lose Augustine either.

The weight of my secrets pressed down, suffocating me. I imagined my husband's face when he discovered the missing funds, the betrayal engraved into his brown features. He'd never forgive me. My mind raced through options: liquidate assets, borrow, beg. Whatever I did, Augustine would notice. He'd dig into our accounts and trace the missing money. And then, the truth would spill out like blood from an open wound.

Outside, rain tapped against the car window. The rainstorm mirrored the hurricane of emotions swirling inside me. I'd danced on the edge of betrayal for too long, and now my son's life hung in the balance as my own sins threatened to unravel everything.

———

As soon as I stepped into the house from the rain, I slipped off my shoes while Augustine brought our suitcases from the trunk. I hurried to our bedroom and closed the door behind me.

The room felt stifling, the walls closing in on me as I paced with the phone pressed to my ear. The window, adorned with faded lace curtains, offered a view of the rain-slicked street as I waited for Karina to answer my call.

"Come on, pick up, Karina," I muttered, my lover's name a desperate plea. But the line stayed silent, mocking my desperation. *Where is she when I need her the most?*

The carpet underneath my feet felt worn, its fibers frayed thin by my restless pacing. I'd traced circles, back and forth, across its faded pattern. I continued to pace, my footsteps echoing like a guilty confession. I glanced at the family portrait on my nightstand, a frozen moment of genuine smiles and happiness. Augustine was handsome and stern, his knowing eyes following me even when he wasn't in the room. Our son, innocent and hopeful, entwined in a moment of childhood bliss. How could I protect him when my own sins threatened to unravel everything?

The room spun, and I sank onto the edge of the bed. "Voicemail again," I muttered, disconnecting the call.

Karina's absence gnawed at me. *Did she somehow know about the ransom? Is she safe? Or has she vanished, leaving me stranded in this nightmare?* We hadn't spoken since our last night together at the hotel. I'd been trying to put some necessary distance between us, but I needed someone to confide in, to share the weight of my sins. But she remained elusive, and I could hear my husband's footsteps echoing down the hall.

"Fuck," I hissed.

Lincoln's face flashed before my eyes, the sweet brown boy who once clung to my skirts, who now faced a sinister fate. My son, my sweet boy. *How could this happen? How could someone want to harm him?* Half a million dollars was the sum that would save him, but at what cost? Augustine's wrath, our already shaky marriage crumbling, my own guilt swallowing me whole.

———

The bedroom tightened around me like a noose closing in. It felt like a cage. My phone slipped from my trembling fingers, landing on the comforter. Augustine stood there, raindrops clinging to his coat as his brown eyes narrowed on my locked phone. *He knows, Cassandra! He fuckin' knows.*

"What's going on with the money, Cass?" he quizzed, voice sharp, almost accusatory.

He'd always been quick-witted, dissecting the details like a seasoned surgeon. I prayed for a diversion to deflect from my own betrayal.

"I... I know it looks bad, but I promise you there's an explanation for everything."

"I want to believe you, but we're talking about a lot of money here. It's not just a few dollars. Where did it go?"

This is it, the moment of truth. I took a deep breath. "I was going to tell you, but I was scared of how you'd react. It's just that—"

Suddenly, his phone rang, cutting me off. He glanced at the screen, and his expression shifted to concern. "Hello?" he answered. "Yeah. I'll be right out." He ended the call before looking back up at me. "It's Vincent. He's outside with some of the cash. I'll be right back."

I nodded. "Of course."

He exited, leaving our paused conversation in the air, the tension visible. I'd been dreading the conversation, and suddenly, it was inter-rupted by a call. *Maybe it's a sign. No. I can't keep hiding this.* Every-thing was a mess, and I was scared. I was scared of losing him and the consequences of my actions. But we didn't have time for that dance. We needed to save our son and unravel the web of deceit later.

Augustine returned with his phone, a black duffel bag, and a trou-bled look on his face. "I'm back. Tell me what's going on with the money, Cass."

"It's not what you think. I didn't gamble it away or anything like that. It was for—"

Augustine sighed before placing the bag on the bed. "I just want the truth. Whatever it is, we'll face it together, like we always have," he assured me.

My tense stance relaxed following his calm demeanor. I parted my lips to speak and let my words flow. "I–I gave the money to Karina, y-your TA."

His face shifted—a flicker of surprise, then anger as he processed my words. "You did what?"

"She's been having financial issues, plus her father's failing health. I decided to help her out. I know it's crossing a line, but it's done now. I'm sorry. I thought I'd have time to put the money back. A-are you upset?"

He hesitated. "I'm not gon' lie. That's... that's a lot to take in."

"I know, and I'm sorry. Karina was struggling, and I couldn't just stand by. I thought I could help without causing any trouble."

His jaw tightened. "It's not just about the money, Cass. It's about boundaries."

"I know how it must look, but it's not what you think. She's been in a tough spot, and I've become a sort of mentor to her. It was never about crossing lines; it was about helping someone in need."

His brow creased. "A mentor? That's... well, that's generous of you. But you're her therapist first. I don't need to tell you that you need to be careful. It's not just our money; it's our reputation, too," he reminded me.

"I understand, and I didn't mean to jeopardize anything. I just wanted to do the right thing. You know how big my heart is."

"She came to me too, y'know, about needing the money."

I paused. "She did?"

"Yeah. I told her I'd look into a discretionary fund, but when I did, it was all a dead end. So, I get it, and I'm not upset with you for helping. We just need to figure out how to handle this without any more damage to our finances now that I'm leaving the game, Cass."

I nodded eagerly. "I'll do whatever it takes to make this right. I promise. I–I love you," I told him, the words tasting like ashes on my tongue.

"I love you, too."

"How much more money do we need to get what the kidnapper requested?"

He sighed before fixating his glance on the zipped bag on the bed. "Vincent just gave me two hundred and fifty thousand dollars. I've got another hundred thousand here in the safe. Then there's whatever we can withdraw from the banks. If they were taken from the beach house, there's no tellin' if the money I had stashed there is still safe."

My chest deflated as another wave of panic surged through my body. "You know the ATM has limits, and all the banks are closed right now. We can't write a check. I mean, what the fuck are we supposed to do?"

"I know. We'll need to divide and conquer and get as much cash as possible. Then we'll meet back here. I still have Vinny workin' some things for me, and I've alerted our accountant."

Feeling defeated, I sat on the edge of the bed and hung my head low. "I just hope Lincoln's okay. You and I both know he's not cut out for this life."

He stepped over to me and grabbed my hand before squeezing it tightly. "Don't worry, baby. We're going to get them both back safe and sound."

A chill ran down my spine. Lincoln's girlfriend never crossed my mind until *he* brought her up. Suddenly, my anger surged. "Oh, right."

His jaw tightened. "What?"

My gaze bore into his. "I just hope you know Lincoln is our child and *our* business. He's our main priority, not her."

"I haven't forgotten whose son he is, Cassandra. I love him as if he was my own. I always have. But Ava's innocent in all this. She's only in this because she's gotten roped up with our family. So until this shit is over, she's as much of *our* business as he is," he declared, his voice raw.

"*Innocent*?" I laughed bitterly. "Like we are?"

He didn't argue. Instead, he grabbed his coat with determination in his handsome features. We were united by fear and bound by love for our son. Yet, I couldn't help but feel my intuition reignite. It had been gnawing at me for weeks since Karina brought it to my attention. I'd barely gotten away with my own infidelity, so I knew better than to confront him about his. We'd both strayed, both drawn to the forbidden fruit. But now, survival trumped our secret betrayals.

"I'll call you when I'm on my way back to the house with the money," he stated.

I watched him exit the room again, knowing our marriage and secrets would have to wait. Our trip to Paris, the city of love, had all but faded into insignificance.

THE STUDENT

The room was small, its walls bare and stained. A single flickering light bulb hung from the ceiling, casting eerie shadows across the cracked paint on the walls. There were no windows, no signs of life, just the oppressive silence that clung to the air. I felt the rough texture of a cold concrete floor beneath me. Lincoln was to my right. Panic surged through my veins as I tried to move. My wrists were bound and chafing against the coarse rope. My head throbbed, and I tasted blood where the gag in my mouth had been. I wanted to scream, to demand clarity, but fear clamped my throat shut.

Standing before me was Karina. She was a striking woman with eyes like shards of ice and a chilling smile that concealed daggers. Before now, she had always been the shadow in the corner who graded papers and whispered secrets to the walls. I'd never paid her much attention until she'd stepped to me about my relationship with Professor Hill. As my eyes adjusted, I noticed something peculiar. Engraved into the floor near my feet was a faded university logo. It was unmistakable: we were on campus. The realization sent a shiver down my spine. Fear tightened my chest. Questions hung in the air like a noose, and I wondered how I'd ended up there tied, bruised, and questioning every fucking thing. The last thing I remembered before waking up there was being held at gunpoint by Jemal at the beach house. *How did we end up here? Why?*

My thoughts raced, fueling the adrenaline pumping as I assessed my situation. I had to escape, find a way out of this fuckin' nightmare. My wrists burned from the tight ropes. I wiggled my fingers, testing their limits. Escape seemed impossible, but I refused to give up.

"You may want to conserve your energy," Karina stated, dressed in all black.

I paused and shot her a cold glare. "Why?" I gasped, my throat raw. "Why me? Why are you two doing this to us?"

Her lips curved into a chilling smile as she circled me like a vulture. "Money, Little Dove. Cold, hard cash."

"I don't have any money!"

"But your little boyfriend's daddy does!"

"What? I don't know anything about what Professor Hill does!"

She scoffed. "Girls like you get all the luck. Well, it's my turn now. And now, you and that pretty boy beside you are gonna make me and my brother filthy fuckin' rich."

Karina, the seemingly innocent figure who held sway over my academic life, had secrets—dark ones. And I had unwittingly stumbled into her and her brother's tangled web. Her mention of Lincoln instantly made me divert my eyes back over to him. He'd been fading in and out of consciousness and was still losing blood.

"Lincoln? Lincoln, stay up, baby! Fight to stay awake! Open your eyes and fight!"

"A-Ava," he whispered.

"He needs medical attention! Look at him! He's barely conscious. He keeps fading in and out. Please, Karina! One of you needs to help him!"

"We're not doing shit until we have the money!" Jemal confirmed, entering the conversation with a bang. "Kit Kat, shut this bitch up, or I will," he stated.

"Do you two want his blood on your hands?"

Karina shook her head. "You and your poor little bleeding heart. Let's see how quickly your tune changes when I let you in on this important piece of information. The robbery at the beach house, the gunman, and your boyfriend—they're connected," she confirmed.

My breath hitched. "W-what? What are you talking about?"

"He's the reason you're in this mess. It was his idea to stage the robbery with my brother. Things went a bit off script, and now, here we are. So if you wanna pin the blame on someone, look a little closer to home, Little Dove."

I cut her a cold glare. "Why should I believe you?"

"Because it's true," Jemal chimed in. "He hit my phone the first time y'all stumbled onto that safe. He didn't know that shit was there. Once he cracked the code, he let me know there was all types of shit inside. He wanted me to come in, shake the place up a bit, get the shit from the safe, and we'd split it on the backend. But hey, my family gotta eat first."

I twisted my neck back to Lincoln, searching for answers in his eyes. Somewhere along the way, I'd memorized every line of his face, the curve of his lips, the crinkle at the corner of his brown eyes. Now, it was fully flushed with guilt. "I-is this true?"

Lincoln's voice trembled as his eyes pleaded for understanding. "Listen," he began, his voice raw with emotion. "It was *never* supposed to go down like this, baby. You weren't supposed to get wrapped up in any of this. The robbery was supposed to be a simple heist, a way to stack my money and make my moves after graduation so Jemal could pay off some debts. But then things spiraled out of control."

At that moment, everything became as clear as fragile glass. We *both* had secrets. His shoulder brushed against mine, and I flinched. His touch was both solace and betrayal. The warmth of our shared connection turned to frost. Our conversations echoed in my thoughts with half-truths, making me wonder how many lies he'd woven into our past and how many threads my own lies had frayed. I questioned everything. *Was it love or manipulation?*

I studied his face—the guilt and vulnerability impressed into his features. "Why involve me?" I whispered. "Why risk my life?"

Lincoln's gaze dropped, and he clenched his fists. "Because I love you," he confessed. "I thought I could protect you and keep you safe. But Jemal had other fuckin' plans."

Jemal cackled in the background. "Sho' did."

Lincoln took a shaky breath. "I'm so sorry, Ava," he acknowledged, each word laced with regret. "I never meant for any of this shit to happen. But now we're both trapped."

Questions continued to claw at my insides. "And the professor?" I asked. "Did he know about the robbery, too?"

"No."

I shook my head, disbelief crashing over me like a tidal wave. Who could I trust? Not Lincoln, with his honeyed words and false promises. Not Jemal and Karina, who circled me like fresh prey, eyes sparkling with secrets. The dark space held no allies whatsoever. I'd always been a diligent student, but this was a lesson in betrayal I hadn't signed up for. It was as if I'd woken up in an alternate reality. His words clung to me like cobwebs. *Is this a nightmare? A hallucination? Or has my reality fractured?*

I clamped my eyes shut, seeking solace in my silent prayers. *Please, God. Let me survive this.* As a coping mechanism, my mind conjured up images of survival—campus police bursting in and saving the day, allowing me to taste freedom again. But my hope was fragile. I'd been thrust into a dark narrative that I didn't know if I'd ever be able to escape from.

"Daddy must be working overtime to get that half a million," Karina stated, her voice slicing through my thoughts.

"Either that or he's workin' with the fuckin' cops," Jemal added with a cynical scoff.

Professor Hill's face haunted me—how he looked when the truth spilled from his sweet lips. My heart wavered between anger and longing, curiosity and chaos. "What the fuck is your father into outside of the university, Lincoln?" I questioned.

Karina's eyes darkened. "What? No pillow talking after your private sessions? Or were you just another one of his quick fucks?" she probed, dropping a bomb on everyone in the room, me included.

"Ooooh shit," Jemal called out, cackling.

She delivered her final twist, the revelation that shattered my entire world. My heart sank. That bitch wasn't content with money alone. She reveled in tormenting me. Hearing my whispered secrets aloud was a gut punch. As mad as I was knowing that Lincoln had a hand in orchestrating the chaos, I never intended for him to find out about me and his father. I planned to take that secret to my grave, but it seemed like Karina had gone to great lengths to expose the skeletons in my closet.

She turned her attention to Lincoln and curiously tilted her head to the side. "Did you know your girlfriend was your daddy's lover? Yup! And news of their little secret affair spreading around campus could ruin his reputation *and* your family. You've still got another year here. Are you really prepared to walk around campus knowing people are whispering about your father being balls deep in your girlfriend?"

The room crackled with tension.

"Ava," Lincoln's voice trembled. "Tell me she's fuckin' lying."

A part of me figured, *if I'm going to die, I might as well go out telling the truth.* In contrast, the other parts screamed for me to lie and deny. My extended silence spoke louder than any simple yes or no answer could, prompting him to follow up with additional questions and accusations.

"I can't fuckin' believe this shit! You got me pourin' out my fuckin' heart to you knowin' you were fuckin' my father? How long has this shit been going on? Huh, Ava?"

I couldn't have been happier that he was restrained at that moment. My gaze dropped to the floor.

"Look at me! How many times did you sleep with my fuckin' father, Ava?" Lincoln repeated, his tone unrelenting.

I sighed. "It—it started innocently. I would write about him in my poems. Then, I'd start lingering after class to ask questions and discuss the literature. But then—"

"But then?" His voice cracked. "Don't you dare sugarcoat it. Tell me the fuckin' truth! How long were you fuckin' him behind my back?"

My breath hitched. "Maybe a few weeks to a month. It—it was never supposed to keep happening. We both got carried away!"

Lincoln's anger surged. "*Carried away*? Bitch, you betrayed me! And with my father! Are you in love with him? Is that it?"

I hesitated, torn between guilt and defiance. "Love? No. It was—"

"What? Convenient?" Lincoln spat, drawing his own conclusions. "A forbidden thrill? Did you think you could keep this shit hidden forever?"

"No! Lincoln, you have to understand—"

"*Understand*?" His laughter was bitter. "You better pray we make it out of this shit alive because if we do, just know I'm a hundred percent done with your smut ass!" he spat.

Tears blurred my vision. "Lincoln, I never wanted you to—"

"You never wanted me to do what?" he barked. "To find out? To cuss your fuckin' ass out? You think this is about what you want, bitch? Do you know what this shit will do to my mother if she finds out? My family?"

I sobbed. "Lincoln, I'm sorry! No one has to find out about this! No one's lives have to get ruined!"

Karina grinned, her eyes gleaming with malice from the pot she'd intentionally stirred. She rested her cold hand on my shoulder, offering false comfort. "There, there, Little Dove. Don't cry."

I snatched my shoulder away, leaning far away from her. "Don't fuckin' touch me!" I hissed.

She scoffed. "Don't get mad at me, bitch. I'm not the villain in your love story. You are."

THE PROFESSOR

The rain fell in a relentless curtain, tapping against the windowpane like impatient fingertips. I stood before the massive painting that adorned the back wall of our walk-in closet. It was an exquisite piece, a hue of vivid colors that seemed to capture both chaos and serenity. But I wasn't interested in its artistic value; I was focused on what lay behind it. My fingers trembled as I pressed against the canvas, feeling the hidden latch give way. The painting swung forward, revealing a steel door. I had installed it myself, a secret compartment where I kept my stash: a stack of crisp hundred-dollar bills. One hundred thousand dollars, to be exact. It was only a piece of my insurance policy, my escape plan from the game, and now it was about to be put to unintended use.

I withdrew the money, counting it meticulously. Each bill repre-sented a sacrifice, years of hard work, and a lifetime of bloody secrets. I placed the cash into the black duffel bag, adding to what Vincent and Cass were able to pull together to get us to the amount we needed. The weight of the bag settled heavily on my shoulders. Cass watched from the doorway, her eyes stark with despair. We'd been through so much together—the good, the bad, and the ugly—but this was different.

"Augustine," Cass finally spoke, her voice a whisper. "Are you ready to make the call?"

I nodded, the gravity of our situation sinking in. To save Lincoln and Ava, we had no choice but to comply. But as I looked at my wife, I wondered if we were making a mistake. I couldn't shake the gnawing feeling in my gut telling me something was wrong. Yet, I persisted. I dialed Lincoln's number back. The phone rang twice before a gravelly, distorted voice answered.

"You got the money?"

"Yes," I replied, my throat dry. "Where do we meet?"

Seconds later, my phone dinged with a text. "And remember any false move, and your son won't see the sunrise," the kidnapper said before ending the call.

They'd sent an address—a location that sent a chill down my spine. It was the university campus where Cass and I both worked. Cassandra glanced at me, her eyes wide with realization when I shared the address with her.

"What the fuck is going on, Augustine? Who's behind this?"

"I don't know, but we're about to find out," I replied before grabbing my gun from the nightstand.

We stepped out into the rain, the cold drops clinging to our skin like icy fingers. I held the duffel bag tightly with Cass by my side. As I gripped the steering wheel, the rain drummed relentlessly on the car roof. The desperate, dark skies above seemed to weep for us as if already mourning our defeat. My gun lay heavy against my thigh, a cold reminder of how high the stakes were. Cassandra sat to my right, her silence echoing the unspoken tension. The wheels spun inside my calculated mind. I had always been meticulous and a planner. As we drove toward the university campus, I checked for traffic cameras, my eyes darting from one pole to another. I knew the layout—the blind spots, the hidden lenses. But this was different. This was personal. My call to the police chief was discreet. He owed me favors, debts accumulated over years of secret partnership. I requested an hour's delay on the traffic cameras, enough time to slip in and out unnoticed. I also made sure he had units set out by the interstate exits, by the bridge, and all exit routes to the city. That way, if they got past me, that mothafucka wouldn't get far. The chief agreed, no questions asked.

The address led us to the heart of the campus, rain-slicked streets reflecting the glow of streetlights. I parked the car near an abandoned lecture hall with ivy grown over its walls. It was a few paces from the library. The engine purred like a dark predator. I checked the gun, the weight of it reassuring. I'd never once considered bringing my weapon to campus, but desperate times called for desperate measures. The GPS screen illuminated, casting an eerie glow in the dim interior. There was still a two-minute walk to the destination. I glanced at Cassandra, her eyes reflecting both fear and determination. We had come this far and were about to step into the heart of our worst nightmare. Her trembling hand found mine before our fingers intertwined.

"You wait here in the car," I told her. "I'll go in."

She shook her head. "No! He's our son. I need to see that he's okay with my own two eyes."

"No, Cass. Wait here," I instructed. "I'll call you when it's safe."

Her grip tightened on my hand. "Okay. Be careful," she whispered. "Call me as soon as you have him."

"Okay."

I stepped out into the downpour, my footsteps muffled by the rain. As I inched closer to the building, my senses heightened. I scanned the surroundings, noting the dark corners and the rusted fire escape. The duffel bag, heavy with half a million dollars, pressed against my side. The campus was deserted, the buildings looming like silent guards. If this was a trap, I was walking into it willingly. But I had made the proper preparations—the wiped cameras, the police units waiting, the gun on my waistband. I followed the GPS instructions as the rain blurred my vision, feet shuffling forward until I arrived at the door. It creaked as I pushed it open. The room revealed itself—a dimly lit space. Inside, the stiff air smelled of old water and fear. And there, bound and bruised, were Lincoln and Ava. Her face lit up with hope when she saw me, but fear lingered in her eyes.

"Son," I whispered to Lincoln.

"Dad, I'm so sorry," he replied just as a female dressed in all black approached me, and the world seemed to shrink.

It was Karina, my TA, with her eyes devoid of emotion. Beside her stood a man I'd recognized as one of Lincoln's friends. They favored each other—her brother, perhaps? My racing thoughts jumbled up at the front of my brain, connecting the dots.

My pulse thundered. "*Karina*? What the fuck is going on?" I asked, my voice a hoarse whisper.

Her gaze flickered to the duffel bag, its weight pulling at my shoulder. She held out a hand for it. I hesitated, then noticed the gun he was clutching and handed it over. Her brother retrieved the bag, and the money disappeared into the darkness.

"Open it," she commanded her brother, gesturing to the bag.

He unzipped the duffel with the stacks of cash. He inspected the money, counting it meticulously. "Seems like you've been good little parents," he sneered.

"It's all there?" Karina asked.

"It is," he confirmed.

"You've got your money. Now let them go," I demanded.

"It's not just about the money," Karina confessed.

"Then what the fuck is it about? My wife told me she had already given you the money. Why the fuck would you do this?"

Karina's lips trembled, but she held her ground. "Your wife is a fucking liar," she said, her voice brittle. "She promised me *a lot* more than money. But the highest amount she could offer wouldn't be enough. Not after what she did."

"What did she do?"

"Your wife and I—we've been seeing each other for a year, and she broke my fucking heart!" she yelled, her eyes filled with rage and hurt.

"I already know she's your therapist, Karina."

"Romantically," she continued. "Behind your back. Behind everyone's backs."

Her words hit me like a physical blow. My mind reeled, memories flashing—late nights at work, whispered phone calls, the missing money. Cassandra, my wife, the woman I vowed to love until my dying breath, had betrayed me. And Karina had been her accomplice right up under my nose all along.

"You're lying," I spat. "This is some sick-ass game. You need help, Karina, beyond what money or my wife can give you."

But Karina's eyes were raw with truth as she pointed to the corner, where a tiny camera lens glinted. "Watch and see for yourself," she replied, her eyes never leaving my face. I watched her retrieve a small flash drive from her pocket, its metallic surface glinting in the dim light. "This holds the truth about the woman we both love. About our past."

The laptop sat there, harmless yet menacing. The dark screen illuminated as Karina plugged in the flash drive and revealed a folder named "Insurance." She opened it, revealing a web of subfolders. She clicked on a video file, and the room filled with Cassandra's moans as she palmed the back of Karina's head between her thighs.

Karina's voice broke. "This was our nine-month anniversary. And this…" She paused, opening another file to reveal a series of incriminating text exchanges between them. "Her infidelities, her lies. I've saved it all."

My heart clenched. Seeing my wife's betrayal unfold in front of me in vivid detail was a different torment altogether. Cassandra, the love of my life, had betrayed me. And Karina, the loyal TA she'd suggested to me, held all the cards in her hand. The videos played on a loop, and the woman I loved was entwined with my TA. At first glance, my mind rebelled, refusing to accept the truth. How could Cassandra go from my anchor to an accomplice? But I couldn't deny the sound of her moans. I knew them all too well. *How could she?* Betrayal cut deeper than any blade. The room suddenly felt smaller, airless. Doubt gnawed at me. *Was I blind? Should I have seen the signs?* My mind replayed moments—her suggestion for me to hire Karina, her drunken compliments about another female professor's body, the missing money. Anger surged through me like wildfire, consuming all reason.

My fists clenched. "That's enough."

Her lips curved into a sardonic smile. "You sure? There's months' worth of footage we can sift through."

"I said shut it the fuck off!"

"Fine," she said, pausing the video.

"Why show me this?"

"You see, Professor," Karina murmured. "Your wife's secrets are worth more than words. They're worth your career, your sanity, perhaps even your son and your whore's lives. So, I'll give you the flash drive. You can confront her, expose her. Do whatever you want. But in return, my brother and I are leaving with this cash and everything from that safe. Enough to press the restart buttons on our lives. To vanish."

My rage surged. I lunged at her, fingers curling around her throat. "Bitch, do you know who the fuck I am?" I snarled, squeezing tight.

The sound of a gun cocking against the back of my skull cut through the chaos. I slowly twisted my neck to see her brother standing there.

"Don't make me splatter your fuckin' brains all over these walls," he threatened. "Let my sister go."

"If you a man, be a man and pull the fuckin' trigger. Because if you don't..." I warned, letting my veiled threat linger.

But Karina was prepared. She gasped, clawing at my hands, and then revealed her final card. "Your s-son," she choked out. "He found your safe—the one hidden behind the painting at the beach house. He plotted to rob you, to steal everything."

My grip instantly loosened. My son, the boy I'd raised, also implicated in this web of deceit? It couldn't be true. The walls seemed to close in, suffocating me. I glanced at the laptop, and the damning footage paused on the screen.

"I guess the moral of the story is: trust no one, Professor Hill," Karina whispered, her voice fading. "Not even your own family."

I stumbled back, torn between love and betrayal. My entire family, my wife, my son—had turned against me. Karina and her brother vanished into the rain-soaked night in my moment of weakness, leaving Ava, Lincoln, and myself alone. We were all safe, but our family was shattered. Once a place of learning, the university campus now held our secrets in its crumbling walls. My decision was clear: I would confront Cassandra and Lincoln. But trust? That was a luxury I could no longer afford to spend on them.

THE WIFE

The rain drummed in a rhythm that was both soothing and maddening, a constant beat that blurred the line between reality and my heightened anxiety. I sat there, engine idling, windshield wipers swishing back and forth, tracing invisible patterns across the glass. My view was a watery haze as I strained to see beyond the glass. The dark building loomed ahead, its windows like empty eyes staring into the depths of my soul. My husband had vanished inside, swallowed by the night's shadows, leaving me waiting, wondering, and trying to calm the frantic beat of my heart. Nervousness clung to me like a second skin. My only son's life hung in the balance, and I was powerless. I imagined him inside feeling alone and frightened while waiting for a hero who might never return.

My fingers tapped against the passenger side door. The cold leather of the passenger seat pressed against my thighs, and I shifted restlessly. I glanced at the clock on the dashboard, each second stretching like an eternity. I wondered what Augustine was doing inside. *Is he bargaining for our son's life? Strangling the kidnapper with his bare hands? Or is he dancing with the devil, making sacrifices that will haunt us forever?*

I pressed my hand to the window, feeling the cold seep through my skin. The building loomed ahead, its oversized silhouette distorted by the downpour. I knew the building Augustine had entered all too well. It had my secrets scratched into its walls. It was where Karina and I had our private, impromptu sessions. No interruptions. No cameras. But, as the rain blurred the world outside, I wondered if she was more than just my romantic confidante. Her sweet face haunted me, from the dip of the cupid's bow on her lips to the intensity in her beautiful eyes. She knew the contours of my mind and body. Was she the architect of our orchestrated nightmare? I'd been the puppeteer for so long, pulling the strings and dictating our relationship. *Fuck. Is that the reason I couldn't get her on the phone?* My mind ran through scenarios: betrayal, jealousy, revenge. *She wouldn't get me back like this, would she? Not my son. She wouldn't involve my son.*

I clenched my fists as my husband's orders echoed in my ears: *Wait here.* His voice was stern and unwavering. I knew better than to interfere with the way he handled his business. Yet, my maternal instincts screamed louder than reason. I unclicked my seat belt, slid across the center console, and settled into the driver's seat. Raindrops splattered against the windshield as I gripped the steering wheel, torn between loyalty and misery. I stared toward where Augustine had disappeared, waiting for a sign—a flicker of light or a phone call. The rain was my only companion; its persistence reminded me of time slipping away. I waited with my nerves coiled tight, ready to spring.

But then, as if the heavens themselves took pity, the intensity of the rain began to diminish. The once-angry, heavy raindrops slowed to a gentle trickle. I hesitated, glancing upward with hopeful eyes. It was the break I'd longed for. A brief intermission in the symphony of water. Was it my sign?

I eased the windshield wipers to the lowest setting and locked my fingers back around the steering wheel. When I looked up, I noticed the familiar black duffel bag swinging wildly as Karina and her brother sprinted across the empty lot toward me. The break in the rain and the headlights had allowed me to see them. Panic clawed at my chest as I realized my worst nightmare had come true. *Why the hell did Augustine let them escape? What if he's dead? Are they carrying my son's fate in that bag? What the fuck is going on?*

I couldn't sit idle any longer. I contemplated calling out to her. I also contemplated running them both down in cold blood. Karina had crossed a serious line. The fracture in our relationship was beyond repair.

"I fuckin' hope it was worth it, bitch!" I screamed inside the car as my foot hovered over the gas pedal. I was ready to chase their asses down, then my phone rang, a needed intrusion into the chaos. I snatched it up, heart pounding. "H-hello?" my voice trembled.

"Come inside," Augustine's voice crackled through the line. "He's safe."

Relief surged through me, a flood of gratitude. "Thank you, baby. Thank you so much." I hung up, my breaths ragged.

My husband was alive. My son was alive. The world tilted back into place, likely to fall again but intact for the moment. I killed the engine, flung open the car door, and ran toward the dark building. The rain-soaked pavement swallowed my footsteps as the building loomed ahead of me. I took a deep breath as I stumbled across the threshold, heart an uneven drumbeat of relief and confusion. Whatever awaited me, I would face it head-on.

The room was a picture of chaos—dried blood specks on the cold concrete like morbid confetti and discarded ropes and gags strewn across the floor. My footsteps faltered as I burst inside, eyes darting between the figures in the room. Lincoln stood there, disheveled and bruised, while his girlfriend sat off to the side, still bound. Relief surged within me, but it was short-lived. My son's frightened gaze met mine, and I saw the truth in his eyes. My husband, the man I'd loved and trusted, had his gun pressed to his spine. The world tilted again, and I struggled to find my voice and next breath.

Lincoln uttered a single word, heavy with surrender: "M-mom. P-please h-help m-me."

I turned to my husband, seeking answers. His handsome brown face was hidden behind a mask of fury, lines of hate etched deep in his brow. "Augustine, what the fuck are you doing? Are you crazy?"

Panic clawed at my throat. This wasn't the man I knew, the one who'd held me in the dark and whispered his wildest dreams against my skin.

His scowl deepened. "You thought I wouldn't find out about your affair?" His voice was a blade slicing through the room.

My breath hitched. Betrayal hung heavy like a noose around my neck as my heart plummeted to my feet. The room spun, and I stumbled back, clinging to the door frame for support. My thoughts sprinted, memories colliding into one another like shattered glass. Not only had Karina siphoned money from my family, but she'd also gone and told him about our affair. *That fuckin' bitch.* I stumbled forward, my voice a fragile plea as I held my palms up in surrender.

"No, baby, please. I don't know what she told you, but it's not what you think."

But my words were useless, drowned out by the storm of accusation across his brow. Augustine's cold eyes bore into mine as his finger tightened on the trigger. I tasted salt—the rain, my tears, a roaring ocean of embarrassment and regret. I knew I'd stepped into the middle of a storm of my creation that would consume us all.

Self-preservation tugged at me. I feared the aftermath of what awaited me on the other side of the truth. I imagined losing my license, the public shame and potential prison bars, and my life crumbling. I owed him my loyalty, but sometimes loyalty came with sharp edges. Survival whispered in my ear, *Choose yourself.* That settled it. I would lie like a rug and pray my woven web of deception shielded me.

"Augustine, listen to me. She's my patient, okay? She's on medication for her depression. She's not mentally there right now, and I just comforted her. Did I overstep some boundaries with the money and things? Yes. I'll admit to that, but that's all it was, baby. You have to believe me."

"Don't play games with me. I've seen the truth, and now you will, too."

"W-what?"

"Go shake the screen."

"Augustine, what is it?"

"Go!" he barked.

My step stuttered forward toward the laptop. On the side of it was a flash drive. I shook the mousepad, and the screen flickered to life, revealing multiple videos of Karina and *me* in more than one compromising *situation*. She'd set up a hidden camera inside our secret space. Defeat hovered over me. The videos were irrefutable proof. I knew I was cornered.

As the videos played, I looked over my shoulder. Augustine's eyes held hurt, anger, and disappointment. I knew he'd never forgive me. The consequences loomed over me like a cloak. I thought about the legal battle, the nasty divorce, my reckoning. Too many lies had spilled from my lips, each one digging me into a deeper grave.

My voice cracked. "Baby, it's not what you think. Karina and I—"

His bitter laugh sliced through my words, cutting me off. "Are what? In love? Is that what you were going to say?"

"Please listen. It's complicated. I—"

"Complicated? You've been sneaking around, lying to my face! And now, the real question: Did you tell that bitch about my business dealings?"

"I... I didn't—" I stammered.

"Another fuckin' lie!"

Tears flooded my eyes. "Augustine, I love you. Karina's in love with me, but I don't love her. She's..."

"A snake. She's the one who's been feeding you secrets, hasn't she?"

"I thought... I had to know if..."

He pointed at the screen with his free hand. "Look! There you are, kissing her, whispering sweet nothings. And there's another one where you're discussing my deals. You betrayed me, Cass."

My voice cracked. "Baby, I never wanted this. Karina was getting too attached, and I'd done everything in my power to try and wean her, but now I know she's behind all of this. She's trying to ruin us, ruin me!"

"You still chose betrayal over loyalty. That's not on her. That's on you. Which tells me that our marriage ain't mean shit to you."

I hung my head, defeated. The room felt suffocating. My heart galloped as fear gnawed at my insides. Fear of losing my husband, my son, and our lives together as we knew it.

The Stepson

The walls seemed to close in on me. My father's warm breath brushed against my ear as he pressed the silencer of the gun harder into my spine. My heart galloped like a wild stallion, and I'd lost control of the reins. *How the fuck did it come to this?* Betrayal, secrets, and desperate choices that would haunt us all forever.

"Why?" His voice was a low growl, his tone dripping with venom. "Why the fuck would you steal from me, Lincoln?"

I swallowed, my throat dry as desert sand. The weight of my guilt bore down on my shoulders. I'd thought I was clever, setting up the robbery to empty that safe, believing I could escape the consequences. But, with the cold steel of my father's gun digging into my spine, I realized how fuckin' foolish I'd been.

"I—I was going to send some to m-my father in p-prison. I... I'm sorry," I stammered, knowing whatever excuse I could cook up wouldn't be good enough.

"What?" my mother yelled out.

His laughter was bitter, echoing off the walls. "*Sorry?*" he spat the word like a curse. "You think that justifies your betrayal? You're my son, Lincoln. Flesh and blood couldn't have made us closer."

I glanced at Ava, a silent witness to our twisted family drama. My mother's face flashed with disgust. She'd always been my confidante, my protector. But she'd kept her share of secrets, siphoning money to fuel her affair with Karina.

"You've been talking to him behind my back?" my mother quizzed, eyes boring into mine.

"It's not what you think. I just wanted to understand, to know who he is."

"What the fuck is there to know, Lincoln? He abandoned us and left me to raise you alone. And now I find out you're cozying up to him and giving him money?"

"You never told me why he's in there! What he did! I needed answers. I needed to know why he chose prison over us."

Her glare sliced me in half. "Answers? You think his ass deserves your sympathy? He's a stranger, Lincoln! A ghost from our past that just so happens to share your DNA! You were practically a baby when he left."

"Mom, I'm not choosing sides. I just want to know him."

She shook her head in disapproval. "You're unraveling everything! He's not entitled to anything! No money! Nothing! You hear me?"

Augustine butted into our conversation. "Enough about your secret prison pen pal! Ain't nobody else gettin' my money without my fuckin' permission!"

"I didn't give him anything!" I yelled.

"Did you know?" his voice dropped to a dangerous whisper. "Did you know your fuckin' mother was stealing from me too? Funding her lesbian lover's escapades?"

My mind raced. I'd always looked at my mother as the gentle soul who'd tucked me in at night after whispered bedtime stories. Yet, she'd betrayed my father, and I'd betrayed them both.

"No," I choked out. "I swear, Dad. I didn't know."

"He's not lying! No one knew!" my mother yelled out.

"What about your girlfriend? Did she have anything to do with it?"

I drew in a deep, trembling breath. As badly as she'd betrayed me, I didn't know which of our hands was the dirtiest. "N-no. S-she was in the dark the whole time."

"You wouldn't lie to me, would you, Miss Newman?" he challenged Ava.

"N-no. We were t-together when we first found out about the safe, but I didn't know he opened it. Honest to G-God, I'm telling you the t-truth!" she answered quickly.

The gun pressed harder, and I tasted the metallic tang of desperation as tears soaked my face. "Dad, I swear I didn't know!"

"Pathetic," he spat, the word venomous. "You think tears absolve you, mothafucka?" His voice, usually measured, scraped against my eardrums like nails against a chalkboard. "Ignorance is no excuse. You're still a disgrace to this fuckin' family."

The room quivered under the weight of my father's rage. My fists clenched, and unclenched, knuckles pale with fear. I'd seen him angry over missed curfews and broken promises, but this anger was different. This was the core of him unraveling, threads snapping one by one. As cold as his words were, I wondered if he'd ever loved me.

"P-please give me a s-second chance, Dad. I s-swear I'll n-never d-do anything l-like this a-again!"

"A second chance? Why would I grant you another chance when you squandered your first? I trusted you, Lincoln. I trusted *both* of you. Not only did you fuckin' lie to me, but you stole from me. Those are the traits of my enemies, not my family!"

"Augustine, please!" my mother screamed. "I'm sorry! We're *both* sorry, okay? But let's be clear: none of our hands are clean."

He shifted the gun from my back and placed it in my hand. I instantly felt the metal cool against my palm. "You want a second chance, son? Prove your loyalty," he commanded.

I blinked, confusion and fear warring within me. "How?"

And then, with a roar, he thrust the weapon toward my temple. "Choose." His voice boomed like a thunderclap. "Your life or your lyin' ass mother's."

The room spun. His request hung in the air like a death sentence. *My mother?* The one who'd kissed my scraped knees when I was a kid, who'd nursed me back to good health when I was sick. I closed my eyes as my father's unthinkable ultimatum echoed louder than my heartbeat. *Choose.* I saw my mother's tear-streaked face and her trembling hands. I saw my reflection—a traitor, a coward. I could save her, sacrifice myself. But how could I be sure that choosing her would lead to my redemption?

I met my father's cold gaze, falling into the abyss within them. And then, with a response that surprised even me, I whispered, "My mother. I choose her."

His lips curled into a snarl. "So be it. Live with your choice."

"W-what?"

My father's grip tightened around my hand as he stood behind me and lowered the gun from my temple to my mother's chest. Then, I realized redemption was a currency he didn't possess. I walked straight into his trap. My choice wasn't between which life I was going to save. It was which life I was going to take.

"Since you wanna be a grown ass man and make grown man decisions, I'ma show you what it takes, mothafucka. Let me see if you got what it takes to take a life, no matter who's staring down the barrel of your gun."

"Dad, no, please!" I begged.

His gaze bore into mine, ice and fire, a contradiction. "Shoot her, or I'll shoot you!" he threatened.

"What? No! What? No! Pop, please. I'm sorry!" I sobbed.

My mother screamed. "Augustine, no!"

I looked ahead at my mother, my tears blurring the edges of her form. "Dad, please."

"This is a valuable lesson, son. Life doesn't give a fuck about your pain, lil nigga. It's merciless, and you need to toughen the fuck up!" he barked as he released the safety. "Do I need to count to three?"

"I'm so-s-sorry, Mom."

She nodded, eyes pleading. "It's okay, baby."

"Dad, p-please don't make me do this. Please!"

"Pull it!" he commanded.

I closed my eyes and squeezed the trigger. *Pow!*

My breath hitched. I'd never shot anyone before. Never in my wildest dreams did I think my mother would be the first life I took. He removed the gun from my grasp, and I breathed a sigh of relief. I opened my eyes just in time to see my mother's body thud to the ground.

Crimson spread across her white peacoat. I sank to the floor, weak with grief. My mother's fear-stricken face swam around my head—the woman who'd given me life. I crawled over to her, clinging to the memory of her warm touch.

"I'm so sorry, Mommy. I'm sorry. I'm so sorry. I love you." I bawled.

My father stepped over to us, the gun clutched in his hand. His face, once a portrait of stern authority, was contorted into something primal, a deadly fusion of fury and betrayal. His jaw clenched, the muscles tight like steel cables. Veins pulsed at his temples, a roadmap of wrath. The brown of his eyes had darkened to a black abyss, devouring any trace of sympathy. His breaths came in ragged bursts, each exhalation a declaration of war.

"Stop lyin', boy. You don't love anybody but your goddamn self!" he spat before aiming the gun at me.

"Please, Dad!" I begged.

He stood over me and grumbled his final words before pulling the trigger. "You broke my trust, which is worse than breaking my heart."

Pow, Pow!

THE STUDENT

I n the midst of it all, I found myself bound and helpless. My heartbeat became a frantic drumroll, each galloping thud pressing through my chest. My breaths were loud and ragged, shallow gasps revealing my terror. Professor Hill had just fired two shots, leaving Lincoln's lifeless body sprawled on the cold floor. I watched him lying beside his mother, bleeding out. The gunshots—the popping sounds that had torn through the silence—still echoed in my ears. The room felt suffocating. It was as if the walls were closing in, pressing against my skin. The ropes that bound my wrists and ankles chafed my skin, leaving angry welts as I fought against them. My veins pulsed with adrenaline. I'd witnessed too much. If he'd murdered his own family in cold blood, I had no reason to believe I wouldn't be next. My life, filled with unful-filled dreams and true love unspoken, flashed before my eyes in a terror-izing flash.

When my tear-filled eyes met Professor Hill's, a cocktail of emotions surged within the depths of me. Fear clawed at my chest as he stepped back, the gun still in his hand. But it wasn't the fear of him, what he'd done, or what he might do to me. It was the fear of the unknown. My thoughts raced, a frantic carousel of dangerous assumptions. Who the hell was Professor Hill outside of West Bridge University? What was his connection to the darkness that had enveloped us all? Why had he been the one to save me from my nightmare? His eyes, sharp and determined, locked onto mine, and the taste of terror clung to my tongue. His gaze held secrets I wouldn't dare comprehend. Yet, I felt a surge of unexplainable peace—his presence, as mysterious and deadly as it was, felt like a second lifeline.

"Listen to my voice," he whispered, his tone steady and soothing. "I won't hurt you, Little Dove. You're safe now."

I clung to his hoarse voice as if his words were the last piece of sanity I had. He untied the ropes with skillful hands, each movement deliberate and precise. His touch was a mix of warmth and ice. As his fingers grazed my skin, I felt a shiver—a tremor that defied explanation. His touch was gentle yet firm as if he held the weight of the world in his hands. The ropes that had bound my wrists had left angry welts, but Professor Hill's touch seemed to erase them. His fingertips traced the contours of my wrists, leaving an unspoken trail of reassurance. As the last knot came undone, he stepped back. I studied him with awe and suspicion etched across my face. I felt a strange sense of gratitude wash over me. He'd saved me, but at what cost?

He reached for me, pulling me to my feet. "Why?" My voice trembled as I slowly found my footing. "Why did you save me?"

Professor Hill's lips curved into a half-smile. "Because some secrets are worth protecting," he replied cryptically.

"I won't tell a soul."

"I know."

Once steady and sure, his hands trembled as he gently wiped my tears away. He dug in his pocket and pulled out a small matchbox. My eyes widened as he struck the match. We stood in silence, watching its tiny flame dance in the darkness. He tossed the match onto Lincoln, and his clothes caught fire. Together, we slipped through the door. Professor Hill knelt beside me, his deadly secrets—the bodies of his wife and son —burned in the crackling inferno.

"What do you do, Professor?" I blurted out, my curiosity overpowering my fear.

I searched his face for answers. He hesitated, then leaned in, his breath warm against my forehead. Before I could process my next sentence, he pressed a gentle kiss against my forehead. His kiss only deepened the mystery, leaving me trembling. Then, he slid a phone into my quivering grasp with a fluid grace. "Wait until I'm gone, and then dial nine-one-one," he instructed.

I watched as he retreated into the shadows, his dark silhouette fading under the cold curtain of rain. I felt the absence of his touch like a phantom ache. His departure was both a relief and a loss. I looked back at the building, watching the fire erase all traces of his existence and secrets. The world wouldn't know of his twisted family secrets, or our sins laid bare. I couldn't help but wonder if forgiveness existed beyond the grave and if I'd ever see Professor Hill again. He'd come into my life and left behind a trail of unanswered questions and a final kiss that felt like a mix of salvation and secrecy. I watched the flames dance for a few seconds, giving him time to escape. Soon, the entire building was ablaze. The phone trembled in my grasp as I dialed the emergency number, my voice shaky but bold.

"Nine-one-one, what's your emergency?"

EPILOGUE

The Professor

Three days later.

Dear WBU Lion Community,

It is with a heavy heart that I share the news that one of our students, Lincoln Adams, and his parents, Doctor Cassandra Hill and Professor Augustine Hill, were declared officially deceased as a result of injuries suffered in the building fire on the north campus a few days ago. The building was fully engulfed in flames when crews arrived, and the three were found unresponsive when firefighters pulled them from the fire. Their tragic passing has left a lasting void in our academic community that cannot be filled.

As we grapple with this profound loss, let us remember Lincoln and his family's impact on our campus: Lincoln was a star basketball player who touched the lives of many of his fellow Lions in ways both on and off the court. His laughter echoed in the quad, and his kindness uplifted those around him. Professor Hill was a scholar who ignited curiosity among his students. His passion for teaching extended beyond the classroom, touching the lives of countless WBU Lions. Doctor Hill championed mental health awareness. Her door was always open, and she encouraged students to seek help when needed.

In the coming days, we will hold a memorial service to celebrate their lives. Details will be shared via email and posted on our university website. Students who need support during this challenging time are urged to call WBU Counseling Services. Support is available to staff and faculty through the Employee Assistance Program.

With deepest sympathy,
  Dr. Zulia White
  Interim President, West Bridge University

My life had been a web of lies woven with dark threads of blood and betrayal. Yet, everything changed the night of the fire. I had Vincent working on the backend to arrange my flight to Anguilla. I had to lay low, and my safe house near the Caribbean Sea was the perfect place. Its existence was known only to a select few. My flight out of the country was a ballet of false identities. I slipped through customs like a ghost in plain sight. I breathed a sigh of relief when I received a call from Chief Wilkinson at the gate. His units had caught Karina and her brother before they could escape the city and retrieved my money and everything they'd stolen from my safe. I instructed him to work alongside the morgue attendant, who owed me a favor. They needed to find another body with my height and build to make the world believe I'd been reduced to ashes and smoke along with my family. To make it stick, I made sure I left behind my wallet for the authorities to find.

It didn't even take forty-eight hours for the headlines to pour in. *Emergency Crews on the Scene of a Fire at WBU* and *Fatal Campus Fire Claims the Lives of WBU Student and Faculty.* I'd orchestrated my demise. A staged accident, a charred body, and a meticulously forged death certificate were all designed to sever the ties that bound me to Potomac Falls. My students would mourn, my colleagues would whisper, but the world would move on.

————

My first morning in Anguilla, I woke up to the gentle lullaby of the sea. Bright sunlight filtered through the sheer curtains, painting the room in hues of gold as the drapes swelled with fresh air from the private balcony. I blinked, disoriented, and then remembered: I was alive, and life as I knew it would forever be altered. Yet, the island welcomed me with azure waters and swaying palm trees, a paradise that masked my secrets.

My safe house was nestled on the island's southwestern coast, perched atop a rocky cliff and hidden away from prying eyes and danger. My nearest neighbor was a half-mile away, a reclusive, old fisherman named Elias who wore linen shirts and walked around barefoot. Its walls were a cool white, offset by wooden accents. Floor-to-ceiling windows throughout the house framed my uninterrupted views of the Caribbean Sea. Its back door opened directly onto a secluded stretch of clean beach, where the sand was as soft as a blade of grass. The house was a fortress disguised as a haven. Cameras, motion sensors, and biometric locks guarded my secrets. My fingerprints were the only keys. In case of emergency, the underground panic room led to an escape hatch to the cliffs below.

I padded barefoot across the cool tiles, the salt-kissed breeze enveloping me like a sweet embrace from Mother Nature herself. But as the sky bloomed with bright hues, I felt a twinge in my chest. Regret, perhaps? Not for faking my death, which had been necessary, but for the collateral damage. Ava, my Little Dove, believed I was gone forever. I'd kissed her forehead and vanished into the night. The ache of her confusion gnawed at me, even as the sun painted the world in its warm glow. Did I feel remorse? Of course. But I also felt alive. Truly alive. For the first time in years, I could breathe without the weight of expectations. I was finally free from the ploys of power and the hollow respect from the game.

I thought of her in the quiet corners of my mind, where memories lingered like old photographs and unhealed wounds. I wondered if she mourned me. If the weight of my absence lingered in the corners of her mind. I'd set her free for a good reason. Ava was a free spirit who wore her youth like a silken gown. And I was a man of responsibilities with a mortgage, career, and a dark past that clung to me like a shadow. I knew we could never be together. Our worlds would remain parallel, intersecting only in the realm of my private thoughts. She was my bittersweet muse, the beautiful ache that lingered when the night was too quiet, and the crashing of the waves couldn't settle me. I sat on the deck, toes buried in sand, and raised an invisible glass to the sky to Ava.

"Spread your wings, Little Dove," I whispered to the sun, knowing there'd always be a special place etched in my heart for her.

———

The Student

Four weeks later.

My alarm rang at seven o'clock sharp. I stirred in my bed, my heart fluttering with excitement and nostalgia. *Today's the day. You fuckin' made it to graduation day!* Golden rays of sunlight tiptoed through my curtains, casting a warm glow across my empty dorm room. Bittersweetness settled over me as I looked at the cardboard boxes stacked by the door, waiting to be unpacked in my new apartment. A job offer far from Potomac Falls awaited me. My gaze shifted to the cap and gown hanging on the door. The black fabric and emerald green scarf held memories of years of caffeine-fueled late-night study sessions, grueling essays, and forbidden secrets forged in lecture halls. The emerald and gold tassel dangled, eager to be moved from right to left, the long-awaited shift from student to graduate.

I sat up, rubbing my eyes and glancing at my phone. The screen illuminated with a cascade of messages. My sisters had beaten my parents to it—congratulatory texts filled the screen, emojis dancing alongside heartfelt words. Vanessa, always the early bird, had sent a GIF of confetti raining down at six o'clock in the morning. Jasmine's message was more composed, but the pride in her words was unmistakable.

Jas: *"Congratulations, Grad!* 🎓 *You did it! We're so proud of you!"*

My heart swelled with joy as my parents' messages soon followed. I quickly replied, thanking them and promising to see them later. I got up and started getting ready, ensuring I was picture-perfect from head to toe. Yet, as I slipped into my gown, my thoughts shifted to Professor Hill. It was the first time I'd felt like an actual dove, ready to spread my wings and fly into the unknown.

I'd done my best to put the events of the day from hell to the back of my mind and lock them away. When the news came out that *three* bodies had been found inside the burning building, I knew something was up but didn't care to question it. After sparing my life, I'd watched Professor Hill disappear into the night with my own two eyes. Yet, if it weren't for the nightmares, it would be like he never existed. Karina and her brother, Jemal, got caught trying to escape the city.

Their getaway car was searched, during which investigators recovered the stolen cash, the gun, and sixteen rounds of ammunition. Turns out, Jemal was a suspect in an open narcotics investigation being conducted by the Potomac Falls Police Department. Him being in possession of a firearm and ammunition was a match made in judicial heaven. The police recovered their phone records and texts linking them to the beach house robbery, kidnapping, and extortion. With all that evidence stacked against them, it was nothing for the cops to charge them with the fire that killed Lincoln, his mother, *and* Professor Hill. They were both in jail awaiting sentencing. The mirror held my reflection. My dark hair cascaded down my back in loose waves, and my eyes were bright with wonder. My smile sparkled with pride and relief as I adjusted my cap.

"You did it, Ava," I whispered to my reflection.

———

Outside, the campus buzzed with anticipation. The air smelled of blooming flowers and freshly mown grass, and in the distance were the sounds of the WBU marching band practicing before the ceremony. I took a deep breath, anticipating the events of the day. I'd walk across the stage, diploma in hand, and step into my future. The journey had been long, but the destination was worth every step. I joined the stream of caps and gowns, standing alongside my fellow graduates. Their hopeful faces mirrored mine. My phone continued to buzz with an influx of love from family and friends.

The Yard had been transformed into a bustling theater where families and friends gathered, their excitement contagious. Black robes with emerald-green hoods dotted the landscape as we all stood tall, ready to walk across the stage. The crowd, a sea of proud parents, siblings, and mentors, erupted with screams and cheers as the procession began. The green and gold WBU banner fluttered in the breeze as the marching band's notes echoed through the air. The mascot, Leo the Lion, danced, embodying the spirit of the university. We marched forward, tassels swaying and hearts thumping. Cameras clicked, capturing every moment. Ahead of us stood our professors in their academic regalia with a vacant chair in memory of Professor Hill.

The stage awaited me—my epic finale. Names were called, and applause and cheers erupted from the crowd. Each step closer to the stage felt weighty. The tassels of graduates before me shifted as they grasped their diplomas. As I stepped onto the stage, I gazed into the sea of smiling faces, and there *he* was. The world narrowed to a spotlight around him. The applause faded for the person ahead of me, and I kept my gaze locked onto a familiar face, a face carved into my curves like ink on paper. Professor Hill stood there, his salt-and-pepper beard catching the light, eyes crinkling at the corners. He'd been presumed dead to the world for weeks, and yet, there he was, standing in the sea of faces with his eyes fixated on me. My breath hitched. It was like seeing a ghost. Then I heard my name: *"Ava Michelle Newman."*

As I reached the center of the stage, the professor's lips curved into a knowing smile. My fingers brushed the diploma before shifting my tassel. The applause swelled, but my gaze remained locked on Professor

Hill. I mouthed a silent "thank you," and Professor Hill nodded—a subtle affirmation. And as I stepped down from the stage, Professor Hill faded into the crowd. I clutched my diploma tightly while walking toward my family, heart full.

———

The air buzzed with excitement after the commencement ceremony ended. Graduates, their families, and faculty members mingled, laughter echoing through the courtyard. As the crowd started to thin out, my eyes sought a familiar face. There he was, standing by the fountain—Professor Hill. His salt-and-pepper hair caught the light, and his tailored suit accentuated his broad shoulders. There was a fedora and a pair of aviator sunglasses covering his eyes. With the mix of people from all over visiting campus and the bouquet of roses in his hand, he easily blended in with the crowd. My heart swelled with butterflies as I approached him.

"Little Dove," he said, his voice warm and deep. "Congratulations."

My smile widened. "So it was you I saw in the crowd. I thought I was seeing a ghost."

"Maybe you still are."

"Well, ghost or not, thank you."

He handed me a bouquet of long-stemmed white roses. Their petals lay against the fabric of my graduation gown. Tucked within the blooms was a small card.

"Open it," he urged, brown orbs twinkling. "A little graduation gift."

My fingers trembled as I unfolded the card. The words were elegant, written in his familiar script:

My Little Dove,

In celebration of your achievements, I've emailed you instructions on how to access the offshore bank account I set up for you. Consider it a nest egg—a start to your beautiful life beyond this university. Don't spend it all in one place.

. . .

With admiration,
A.H.

My breath caught as I glanced up at him, eyes wide. "Professor, I—"

He placed a finger on my lips, instantly silencing me. "Loyalty is a mothafucka. Promise me you'll soar, Little Dove."

I nodded, tears shimmering. "I will."

He leaned down, brushing his lips against my forehead. His gentle touch was fleeting, yet it held a lifetime of unspoken emotions. Then, with a final smile, he melted into the dispersing crowd, leaving me clutching the bouquet and the promise of a future he had quietly given me.

————

Later that night, I sat on my bed. The bouquet of white roses was still fresh in a vase on the windowsill. The scent of their petals mingled with the weight of the moment. Professor Hill lingered on my mind like a dark, twisted fantasy. The simple, unassuming card was his parting gift. I traced the handwriting with my fingertips. He'd always been cryptic, veiling his wisdom in metaphors. But faking his death and risking everything to show up at my graduation? It was beyond anything I could fathom.

My heart tugged toward the unknown. I checked my email, found the bank account's login information, and tapped enter to log in. The screen blinked, confirming the impossible truth: one-million dollars. The professor's gift wasn't just money but a second lifeline. I would invest wisely in art and real estate. I'd travel and see the world. With a million dollars, the world was my oyster. That money–gifted to me by a ghost from my past–was a release from all my financial shackles. Although Professor Hill had vanished, I still felt his presence—how he'd call me Little Dove. It wasn't just about money; it was about flight. The million dollars were my wings, a leap into a fresh life, and a chance to pen my next chapter.

THE END

Afterword

A note from K.L. Hall.

Reader,

Thank you for reading "Professor Zaddy: A Potomac Falls Novel." If you've made it this far, I hope you'll consider telling me what you thought about the book in the form of a **five-star review and/or rating**. Don't hesitate to let me know what you'd like to see from me next! I thoroughly enjoy reading your thoughts and hearing from you as well! I'm always striving to attract new readers and retain current ones, and reviews are one of the easiest ways to attract readers. If you loved the book, tell a friend, and most importantly, let me know!

All my love,
K.L. Hall

About the Author

K.L. Hall is a national bestselling and award-winning author. As a serial storyteller, Hall has penned over three dozen titles in various genres—including African American urban fiction and romance, paranormal, children's books (as Kimberley M.), and non-fiction. Her fictional stories straddle the intersection of classic Urban and spell-binding Romance.

Highly Acclaimed Titles:

In the Arms of a Savage: (Peaked at #1 in Women's Fiction)

The Potomac Falls Series (Peaked at #1 and #2 in African American Erotica)

Sign up for my mailing list to stay updated with new releases, giveaways, sneak peeks, and more! Click this link: https://bit.ly/38RMpV5

Connect with me on social media:

Facebook: https://www.facebook.com/authorklhall

Twitter: https://twitter.com/authorklhall

Instagram: https://www.instagram.com/officialklhall/

Website: https://www.authorklhall.com

Other Potomac Falls reads by K.L. Hall:

Something Bleu

Something Borrowed

Something New

The Knight Before Christmas: A Potomac Falls Short

I'll Be Home for Christmas: A Potomac Falls Short Book II

Triggered: A Potomac Falls Novella

Because You Don't Know My Name: A Potomac Falls Novella
Will You Say My Name: A Potomac Falls Novella Book Two
Remember My Name: A Potomac Falls Novella Book Three
Professor Zaddy: A Potomac Falls Novel

Other novels by K.L. Hall:
Diary of a Hood Princess 1-3
Rise of a Street King: The Justice Silva Story *(Spin-Off to the Diary of a Hood Princess series)*
Broken Condoms and Promises 1-3
In the Arms of a Savage 1-3
Built for a Savage: Blaze and Camille's Love Story *(Spin-Off to the In the Arms of a Savage Series)*
A Ruthle$$ Love Story 1-3
Fallin' for the Alpha of the Streets 1-2
The Most Savage of Them All: The Wolfe Calloway Story *(Prequel to the In the Arms of a Savage Series)*
When a Gangsta Loves a Good Girl
Caught Between My Husband and a Hustler
The Illest Taboo 1-2
To the Only Thug I'll Ever Love
A Lover's Heist: Chief and Gianna's Love Story
A Lover's Heist II: Rome and Lira's Love Story
A Lover's Heist III: Baby and Skai's Love Story
Crushed Velvet & Cashmere
Crushed Velvet & Cashmere 2
Entanglements
Never Had a Bad Boy Love Me So Good
Good Girls Always Got a Thing for the Thugs

Short Reads + Novellas:
Bi-Curious: An Erotic Tale
Bi-Curious 2: Tastes Like Candy
A Savage Calloway Christmas *(Christmas novella to the In the Arms of a Savage Series)*

Lovin' the Alpha of the Streets: A Valentine's Day Novella *(Valentine's Day novella to the Fallin' for the Alpha of the Streets Series)*

Awakened: A Paranormal Romance

As Long as You Stay Down

Solace in Seven

Solace II: The Final Cut

Wasted Off You: A Friends to Lovers Novella

Every Thug Needs a Lady: A Lady and the Tramp Retelling

Ten Things I Hate About Lovin' You: An Enemies to Lovers Novella

In Exchange: An Urban Thriller

Children's Books:

Princess for Hire

Princess Twinkle Toes & the Missing Magic Sneakers

Little One, Change the World

Adjust Your Crown: A Self-Love Coloring Book for Children of Color

Non-Fiction:

Authors are a Business: The Booked & Busy Course Mini Book

BLP

Visit bit.ly/readBLP to join our mailing list for sneak peeks and release day links!

Let's connect on social media!
Facebook - B. Love Publications
Twitter - @blovepub
Instagram - @blovepublications

We hate errors, but we are human! If the B. Love team leaves any grammatical errors behind, do us a kindness and send them to us directly in an email to blovepublications@gmail.com **with ERRORS as the subject line.**

As always, if you enjoyed this book, please leave a review on Amazon/Goodreads, recommend it on social media and/or to a friend, and mark it as READ on your Goodreads profile.

By the Book with B Podcast: bit.ly/bythebookwithb